BB

A PROMISE MOON

2/24/15

Stephen Allten Brown

Stephen Allten Brown

Other books by the Author
Shadows of Chaco Canyon

DEDICATION

In memory of Louis Bruchansky, who gave me back
my name.

ACKNOWLEDGMENTS

Thank you to Anne for her continued support, Amy Brown for her deft editing and Jenny Schroerlucke for her grammatical guidance. A special thanks to all of the people who shared their family history with me during my research.

Cover design and illustration by Anne Milligan

CHAPTER ONE

Rachel pushed aside a corner of the curtain and tilted her head to look outside. A sheet of ice covered the sewage ditch running behind their house, but they were uphill from the collecting pond and most of the smell settled around the houses below them. A barn owl hooted, and the frantic scratching from field mice scurrying for cover slipped between gaps in the floorboards. The other shacks had dirt floors. Enough light from the full moon streamed through the window to cast her silhouette against the wall, and her high cheekbones, full lips, and a thin, graceful neck might have adorned the pyramids instead of the unfinished walls of a slave shack had the era been different.

"Promise Moon, Joe," she said. "This year sure to be better."

I'll be here every time there's a full moon, Grandma had promised. *We'll call it our Promise Moon.* Grandma had held her until she fell asleep, just like Mama did before the slave traders took her away. From that night forward, once a month Grandma had made the long walk to hold Rachel in her arms on the full moon.

"This year sure to be different. Don't know 'bout better." Joe rolled out of bed the way cold honey stretches off a dipper. He interlaced his fingers and stretched the kinks from his back, rubbed sleep from his eyes. He was taller than the bed was long, but he kept his head down and his shoulders hunched forward from habit.

"This a Promise Moon. About the only time good things happen around here." Rachel glanced to where their baby son lay sleeping, saw his breath, like hers, leaving tendrils hanging in the frigid air.

"Promises ain't no match for trouble," Joe said.

"Don't matter. You Massa's favorite. Who he always call when something need fixing?" She could see the muscles in his strong arms through the worn sleeves of his shirt. She remembered feeling safe while wrapped in those arms, but that was a long time ago, when they first vowed to watch over each another. Born a week apart, they shared the same wet nurse and played together in the fields, not realizing that children too small to work were used in the fields to act as scare-crows. Their childhood ended at age five, when they were put to work picking worms off tobacco leaves.

"Massa had him a favorite horse, too," Joe said. "Loved that horse. Cried after he shot it when its leg got broke."

"You and I is different—better. We spend more time in the big house than all the others put together. I practically raised Little Missy. Who she always play with? Me. She even taught me to read."

His shoulders slumped forward until his chin touched his chest. He wouldn't look at her, the way he did when he didn't have anything good to say. "You know that's mostly 'cause the Missus don't like dawgs in the house."

Rachel put her hands on her hips. Leaned over and tilted her head so he couldn't look away. "You calling me a dawg?"

"No." He glanced up at her but quickly averted his eyes. "You more of a pet, really. That child the spit-ting image of her mama and she full of trouble—bell-ringing trouble."

⇒⊱ ⊰⇐

Early the next morning, before the sun was all the way up, Old Shaky rang the bell when it was time for work. He wouldn't ring it again until after the sun went down when he decided it was time to quit, but when he rang the bell in the middle of the afternoon, it meant trouble of the worst kind: bell-ringing trouble. Patches of gray stubble clung to his puffy cheeks. A failed goatee covered part of his chin, and his moustache was no better. He stopped ringing the bell when everyone had gathered outside the big house. His lazy eye made it hard to know where he was looking, but he coiled his whip and turned toward the tree-lined entrance.

A row of slow-growing oak trees lined the drive leading to the main road, and the slaves followed Old Shaky's gaze as he watched a crowd of people materialize from the dust cloud kicked up by their bare feet. Men of all ages, sizes and shades of black were chained together. Women and children followed the coffle, some tied with rope, others merely herded, their terror more effective than chains. Two of the women wore bright red and green scarves and carried baskets on their heads. One man had a bone through his nose. Another man, with blue-black skin, had tribal scars on his face. Armed men riding horses ensured the coffle remained intact.

"Look like they being marched to cotton," Rachel said.

"Being marched to the slow death, more like." Joe crossed his arms and held them against his chest. His large hands hid the holes in the front of his shirt.

"They chained two by two, like they headed for the Devil's ark."

A carriage pulled away from the big house. The house slave who drove the carriage stopped beside the bell tower and tied off the horses. At his master's nod, he set up a writing table in front of the bell, set two chairs behind the table and placed a black leather satchel on top.

Rachel grabbed Joe's arm and backed away from the table. She recognized the satchel. It held last year's bills.

Marse Williams stepped away from the carriage, held up an official-looking paper with fancy marking on it. "All this talk about the Emancipation Proclamation." He wadded up the paper as if it were garbage and threw it on the ground. "This is the first day of 1863, but it's still Kentucky. It doesn't free any of you."

"It doesn't free you," he pointed toward Joe while he ground the paper beneath his boot heel. "Or you." He pointed toward Rachel.

With each grinding twist of his boot, he pointed to another of his slaves. The paper was unrecognizable, yet he continued to grind it into the dirt as he pointed to each slave who comprised the elders and leaders. "None of you are free. None of you are getting free, so don't get any ideas too big for your head." He bent over and set what was left of the paper on fire.

Rachel watched it burn. When the flames died out, Marse Williams stomped on the ashes. Red sparks formed meteor trails until all that remained was a blackened spot in the dirt.

The stranger riding at the front of the coffle dismounted and handed the reins of his horse to the carriage driver. He refused Marse Williams' outstretched hand and sat at the table. Marse Williams ignored the slight and kept his nose in the air as if he were the one doing the buying.

Old Shaky rang the bell a single clang and sidled up to the table: the Devil's disciple ready to deliver damnation. When his whip hand started to tremble, the lash was about to follow. None of the slaves moved. No one spoke. A breathless kind of quiet settled over the courtyard, the hushed silence a field mouse takes on when the hoot from a barn owl tells him he's being hunted.

The slaves eased backward another step but Old Shaky coiled his whip and kept coming. The youngest men and the strongest women of Marse Williams' slaves were added to the coffle—that's what was needed down south. Some of his debts took two slaves to repay, others only one. When the last person was sold, the mourning began.

Rachel was all cried out. It wasn't the first time someone she loved had been sold, and it wouldn't be the last time, either. Unless… She stared at the worn floorboards and crinkled her nose against the peculiar odor of rat feces. *How did I get so prideful about not having a dirt floor when I got field mice living under my feet?* The door wasn't much better, three warped planks held together with a scrap piece of wood. Some of the bark still clung to the knots. No doorknob, just a length of rope knotted on both ends. Instead of hinges, two strips of animal hide kept the planks from falling when the door was open. *So what if we got the best shack or don't got to share it with two other families? Still a shack—used-up wood with a leaky roof.*

Samuel, their first born, started to fuss. Cold, probably, she'd just finished nursing him a short time ago. He'd be walking soon. *And then what? Working in the fields as a scarecrow until he's old enough to pick worms off tobacco leaves. Spending his life in a field with mosquitos so thick, he'd disappear from view if he was more than 10 feet away. That ain't no life.*

Joe picked Samuel up out of the old, rusted-through washtub they used for a crib. The other slaves made do with straw or cut grass and envied their good fortune.

"Up, Dada." Samuel giggled when Joe playfully tossed him in the air.

"This our last chance, Joe," she whispered. "I don't want our baby raised a slave. We got to run."

"But we ain't been sold." He wrapped the gunnysack blanket around Samuel and gently laid him in the tub.

"Yet."

"Maybe never. We different—you the one said it. Besides, been talk 'bout the Union Army. Heard they fighting at Perryville—wherever that is. Suppose to be close."

"Not close enough. Heard the Missus talking 'bout going back to France for more shopping. Marse Williams yelling he can't afford it. Had them an awful row, but she going anyway. Next time that satchel of bills come due, you and me getting sold—bound to happen—ain't that many of us left to sell."

"You talking 'bout France and I ain't hardly been past the last fence. Don't even know how big Kentucky is. Don't know nothing 'bout that Ohio River. What if it ain't the freedom river like everybody say?"

"Then we keep going."

"Where? Where we going? You the one with the top eye, and you don't even know."

"I'm just as scared as you." She held out her hands so he could see the fear shaking in her outstretched arms. "But we can't wait no longer. They bound to start looking at first light."

She reached for her shoes, little more than strips of leather held together with cord. Born a slave, raised a slave, the lash of the overseer's whip was her teacher, the only topic subjugation, the lessons harsh. But the ghosts of her ancestors cried out for her soul. She heard their pleas. The ancestors mourned lost dreams and pleaded with her to avoid their mistakes.

"Ain't got no peace 'bout this."

"Just one step," she whispered. "One little step. Next one gonna be easier."

His feet refused to move.

She slid her foot a few inches toward the door. "See? I'm just as scared as you, but that's nearly a step. C'mon Joe, maybe the next one gonna be easier."

"My feet is stuck to the floor."

"I love you, Joe. Won't be happy without you; can't be happy staying here. We got to go." She lifted their child from beside him. "Don't want our baby raised a slave. That ain't no life."

"And if we get caught? Sold downriver and worked to death? That ain't no life, neither." His coat was within reach, hung on a stick wedged into the gap between the unfinished logs of their shack, but his arms remained at his sides.

"One step, Joe." She wrapped the blanket around Samuel, fashioned it into a simple sling to hold him. She reached for Joe's hand. "One step," she whispered. She held out her hand until her arm became tired. "Just one little step."

He swallowed hard. "Can't move my feet."

"One little step." She refused to lower her arm. He couldn't raise his head.

"Give me your hand."

"Sorry." He didn't look up. "I'm sorry."

"Won't give up on you," she promised. "Not now. Not never. But we got to go!" Her shoulder strained with fatigue until the weight of her arm slowly pulled her outstretched hand to her side.

His gaze remained on the floor.

If she stayed, if she wasn't sold or worked to death, she would see this same splintered wood, smell the rodents living underneath her feet, every day for the rest of her life.

She slid her other foot forward and reached for the rope. *Was Joe right? Was she trading a bad life for something worse?*

You got to stay strong, child, Grandma whispered, but her words took the sound of rain falling on a rusty tin roof.

You got to survive. Grandma helped the wind swirl this reminder beneath a gap at the bottom of the door.

This a Promise Moon. A shaft of moonlight streamed through a hole in the greased paper covering the window and settled on the knotted rope.

It's time to leave, child. The floorboards creaked beneath Grandma's footsteps as she walked across the room. *Open this door. Start a new life.*

"I'm going, Joe. I'll wait for you when I get there, but I'm going where Mr. Lincoln says we can be to-gether and free."

She hesitated. Gave him one more chance, and then turned her back on him. She stepped outside.

Wind fluttered the ragged edges of Samuel's blanket. She pulled the tattered corner over her baby's head and wrapped the remainder across the lower half of his face. He got fussy if he couldn't turn his head to either side and watch what was nearby.

"We headed for freedom, child. Promise we ain't coming back." She shivered. Felt the Devil nearby. The plantation house sat perched on a hill, same as a buzzard. She bent over and crept away from the shack to where a split-rail fence disguised the contours of her shadow. The last section of fence came together to form a "V," so she knelt beside the largest split rail, the worm log resting on the ground. The fence line stopped where the tobacco fields began. She turned sideways, so her profile remained hidden by the overlapping rail. Her shadow disappeared when she leaned into the pole bean runners and peeling bark.

Some folks claimed she had the "top eye," and could see into the future, but there wasn't any trick to seeing something before it happened—it was common sense and the uncommon patience to use it. Her Grandma taught her how to look for the little things most people missed. The big house cook must still be asleep; else, there'd be the smell of yeast in the air. The white folk wouldn't be awake for hours.

The sixth sense her Grandma taught her meant she noticed what was nearby and figured out what it meant. The animals stabled in the barn couldn't see her. They'd keep quiet if she did. But no slave could walk across an open field at night without being guilty of something, and only acres of tobacco plants separated them from a far-distant stand of trees where the land was too rocky to plow.

She ran like the dogs were already after her. Samuel started to cry when the knot tied in his sling worked loose. She placed her hand on the back of his soft head and pressed it against her chest. They were both crying by the time she reached the end of the field. A few scraggly trees provided cover, but these spindly hickories were too full of knots to use for anything but a windbreak.

"Lord!" she whispered, halfway between a prayer of thanks and a plea for mercy. It wasn't safe for them to stay here long, just enough time so she could catch her breath and make sure no one followed. "We on our own, Samuel."

He stopped crying at the sound of her voice, moved his head and kicked his feet. "Dada?"

"Just you and me, child. You got to be quiet. Think I hear the dawgs."

A gust of wind rocked her off balance, the kind of breeze that favors tracking hounds. She had an onion in her pocket to rub on her feet, but dogs could follow the faintest of trails. A bloodhound could track a runaway slave from the scent lingering on a downwind tree. She hunched over Samuel and turned away to keep the wind at her back. The gust passed. She broke off a branch from a nearby red cedar to smooth over signs of their passage. She ground a bayberry leaf between her thumb and index finger and scattered the pieces. The pungent herb would help cover her scent and slow the dogs, but a bloodhound could track through most anything. Grandma taught her about herbs and healing. *But why didn't you teach me bout healing myself? No matter how many times you don't answer, can't help myself asking.*

"We best keep moving, child," she whispered. Samuel appeared soothed somewhat by her voice but squirmed as she pulled the blanket over his head and tucked in the sides. She refashioned the sling and draped it over her shoulder. This time she pulled it tight across her chest and tied the knot below his feet. "Only way I can make sure you don't fall out—just for a little while. You be a good boy and don't cry—the dawgs is loose, I hear 'em coming."

The north wind clumped clouds around the full moon the way a churn chases buttermilk to the top. Not much light to cover unfamiliar ground, but enough. She reached for the nearest tree, a black walnut with serrated bark the width of her finger. She searched between the furrows on the far side of the tree until her fingertips identified a clump of moss with the consistency of an overripe piece of fruit and the soft texture of peach fuzz. This was north, nature's compass. A hundred yards more, and she slid her fingers over the smooth bark of a wild cherry tree devoid of moss. The next tree felt like a ghost tree: a sycamore with peeling bark and eerie white upper branches illuminated by the moonlight. Moss could be tricky, she knew—sometimes growing on the north side but preferring the side of a tree facing the prevailing winds if they carried moisture. The wind swirled around to the west in this river valley. By keeping the moss to her left, she headed north.

A spindly grapevine led to the knotty trunk of a dogwood that guided her to the edge of the small woods. From here the ground sloped toward the river. She heard the soft whisper of water flowing over rocky soil. The river dragged a mass of cold air along with the current and she shivered. *Huh. Mint growing over there. Smells so strong, about ready to harvest…*

The riverbank collapsed beneath her feet. She clutched Samuel to her chest and the back of her head struck the riverbank's rocky edge. She landed on her neck, her chin struck her chest, and Samuel tumbled from her arms.

"Dada!" he wailed, and started to cry. The dogs responded to his cries with angry howls.

"Samuel," she called. *Oh God! Where is he…?*

CHAPTER TWO

The wind carried the excited yips of bloodhounds chasing a scent. Their howls were the sound of the Devil coming to claim another lost soul. Rachel heard the ancestors' sorrowful cries in the thunder; she felt their pain from the whip when she struck her hand against a sharp rock. She cried and her tears mixed with rain. An entire race shed its tears. Her tears joined the ocean, carried to the watery graves of the ancestors.

"Samuel! Where are you?" She screamed, but all that passed through her lips were the desperate wails of a frantic mother searching for her lost child. Grandma's words came back to her: *You got to stay strong, child; you got to survive. Our ancestors drowned—thrown from slave ships. The rain carries their sorrow and the rivers carry the memory of their lost souls.*

"Dada?"

"Samuel? Where are you?" Rachel turned into the wind to pick up his next words.

"Want Dada."

Samuel had landed on a clump of river oats and then slid headfirst to the bottom of a small ledge left behind by retreating flood waters.

"There you are!" She hugged Samuel to her chest. "Joe can't come, baby. Just you and me now."

"No. Want Dada!"

"Just you and me, child. You be a good boy and quiet down."

"Up." He held out his arms for Joe. No one else could throw him in the air and catch him like Joe. It never failed to make him giggle. "Up," he repeated. When Joe didn't come, Samuel's bottom lip turned down the way it did when he was mad. He took a deep breath and screwed up his face to cry.

She held him to her breast and cooed a mother's soothing sounds, but when he got fussy, only Joe or belladonna tea could settle him.

The dogs howled. Their mournful cries meant they'd picked up their scent or heard Samuel's cries. She held him above her head and plunged into the water to wash away their smell. She waded upriver until a curve hid them from view, and then crossed to the other side. She ran until her side ached, ran until fear no longer helped her ignore the pain.

Let it rain, God. Bring a storm like the one you brought Noah.

When she fell from exhaustion, she crawled to the river and huddled in the water. She clutched Samuel to the side of her neck and settled chest-deep in the frigid water, leaned against a steep bank and shielded both of them from view by draping the low-hanging branches of a weeping willow over their heads. Some of the tree roots had been washed out and formed a shallow cave in the riverbank, so she squirmed beneath the overhanging roots as far as she could. Sodden leaves brushed against her face as she pulled a few of the willow's lowest branches over their hiding place.

The dogs splashed in and out of the water where she'd doubled back and run along the far bank to throw them off her trail. They brayed, aware that she and Samuel were close. She heard the hounds scratching and snuffling at the ground. She heard men shouting, cursing; felt splashes when the dogs dove into the water beside her. Peering through the trailing willow fronds, she could see leather boots entering the stream after the dogs. The current carried the sound of their thrashing downstream. They were so close, she could feel the turbulence from their crossing. *Please God, please make a way...*

A bolt of lightning struck nearby and the ground trembled. A second lightning bolt crashed into the willow tree over her head, sending a shock through her body, forcing her head above the water. Fire leapt to the crown of a nearby hickory tree and the bounty hunters retreated. Around her head, the tree roots smoldered. A rending shriek came from overhead and the tree's flaming branches plummeted into the water.

The dogs wailed, howls of pursuit transformed into fatal bellows of pain. God sent a different lightning bolt to sever the five huge arms of a stately oak. The concussive blast from the limbs falling to the earth sent flames sweeping in all directions.

Fire surrounded her. She ducked beneath the water. When the surface of the river felt ready to boil, she pushed off from shore and swam underwater to the middle of the river. Flames consumed the undergrowth along the riverbank and spread to the nearby trees. The current tugged at her clothing. She kicked her legs but couldn't touch the bottom.

"Run!" one of the bounty hunters screamed. Another man's shirt caught on fire. Bright orange and red flames flared from his sleeve and ignited the collar. The water turned muddy as their boots churned up the reddish clay soil on the water's edge. Their splashing stopped and the sound of thudding boots meant they were running away.

The men's shouts continued but grew fainter. The swift current sent her tumbling along the river bottom. She clutched Samuel to her chest, kicked her legs and swept her free arm through the water until the sky above was blue instead of reddish-orange. When she managed to get her feet pointed downstream, she pushed off against the sandy soil and half-lunged, half-swam toward shore. She crawled away from the river and pulled herself upright with the help of a sheltering thicket of river birch.

Lightning brought torrents of rain. High winds made it a storm. A blessing and a curse, the wind made walking difficult but removed their scent from the nearby trees and obliterated all signs of their passage. The dogs would not be able to track them, even if the bounty hunters regained their nerve and control of the hounds. When she could walk no farther, she burrowed beneath a makeshift blanket of leaves. She clasped Samuel to her chest. He didn't protest, didn't ask for Joe. If he was as tired as she was, he was all cried out. There was no reason to awaken him. She was too cold to dream, but Grandma watched over them.

The rain stopped. The wind died down. The bounty hunters found reinforcements, but their torches couldn't cast enough light for a search when a low-hanging fog settled over the valley. Black storm clouds kept the moon from revealing their hiding place.

Grandma crossed over from the other side and sent a fox to run across the trail when the dogs got close to finding Rachel's scent or hearing Samuel's faint whimpers. By the time the bounty hunters found the dogs gathered beneath a tree and baying at the fox, Rachel and Samuel had moved on. One bounty hunter nearly stepped on them at the next hiding place, but Grandma put the taste for a cigarette in his mouth. The flare from a match left him seeing red spots instead of Rachel's silhouette showing through the stunted sumac bush where she was hiding. Grandma was there when the wind rolled a dried gourd in front of a tracker so he heard the percussive sound of seeds hitting a brittle shell instead of the crackle of Rachel's misplaced footstep. A second gust rattled desiccated oak leaves. He cupped a hand behind his ear to listen in the other direction and moved on. When the hounds came back, Grandma brought more rain and thunder. When daylight forced her return to the other side, Grandma brought Rachel the top eye so she could keep running.

Rachel moaned in her sleep, shifted her legs to get comfortable and woke herself. Her top eye was restless. Winter was both friend and foe. Not too hot to travel, but not offering much cover, either. She squinted into the faint light of the coming sunrise. Two areas of flattened foliage and oak saplings stripped of bark told her deer once inhabited these woods.

She'd seen the same patterns in the woods at the forested edge of the plantation. The songbirds were in their nests or far to the south. She trusted their warning calls and sudden silences more than anything else.

She cupped a hand behind her ear. The only sound was of a forest as it settled into a long winter: barren tree limbs that creaked and groaned in a faint breeze.

Her nose itched. Something didn't smell right. She turned into the wind and let the scent guide her. *Maybe a stall needing mucked out. Maybe an uncovered trash pit way past full. Best find out for certain...*

She crouched behind an evergreen bush and scrutinized a simple farmhouse slowly going to ruin. Ivy grew on the walls. Weeds inhabited the flower beds and the bucket from the well lay on the ground instead of suspended from the support. A candle flickered in the windowsill but the curtains on either side were moth-eaten and dirty.

Why's that candle in the center of the windowsill instead of off to the side? And why they lighting a candle when it's daylight? Maybe they forgot—

The flame flickered and went out.

Run? Hide? She held her breath and forced herself to be still and stay silent.

"Son of a bitching bastard! Keep that goddamn candle lit."

The voice came from within the house, so loud and harsh the house's walls barely muffled it. *Bounty hunter!*

I recognize the foul mouth. Ain't nobody can swear better 'n a bounty hunter.

She took a stealthy step backward and put another tree between this compromised house and the forest's edge.

"Goddamn it to hell!" A match flared. The outline of a thin shoulder and scrawny neck crept through a gap in the curtains. The candle was relit and replaced in the center, almost touching the window.

That a signal to avoid this place. Good thing that bounty hunter don't know keeping the candle off center is the safe sign. Where he's got that candle, it's screaming "keep away." And what kind of fool lights a candle when the sun's out? No wonder the deer moved on. Time for me and Samuel to do the same.

A gust of wind sent a few leaves tumbling past the white oak on her right. Desiccated oak leaves chattered overhead. Skeletal strands of switch grass swayed beside her. Rachel heard Grandma's voice when a few seeds shook loose and tumbled out of sight. Thinking maybe Grandma would put in a good word with God since it was the Sabbath, she prayed.

Ain't particular, Lord. Show me a way.

"Amen," she whispered, and before she could get off the ground, she felt the wind shift in answer to her prayers. She followed the breeze, but every step carried her further into the unknown.

She kept the river to her left. This was north. Sycamore trees growing along the floodplain offered limited cover and marked the lowlands where there was water. Chokecherries still had their bright red fruit, so sour the birds refused to eat them until late in the winter when nothing else was left. She couldn't afford to be so particular. Samuel was nursing, but unless she had something to eat, her milk would give out. Exhaustion settled onto her body but her spirit longed to be free. She kept walking, only stopping to listen for danger. The bounty hunters were out there, watching—tracking. She stayed ahead of the dogs by risking travel during daylight and not stopping at night.

CHAPTER THREE

Rachel found a patch of wild onions on the morning of the second day. She forded the river late in the afternoon where an oxbow had formed. Cattails grew in the marshy lowlands left behind when the river changed course, and the base of the stems could be eaten raw if they were chewed long enough. She foraged enough food to chase away the hunger pains and chewed on wood sorrel to anesthetize the sores forming in her mouth from a poor diet.

She stopped and crouched in the middle of a tall stand of river oats to nurse Samuel. He was fussy because her milk was giving out, and if she didn't get some food in her stomach soon, neither of them would survive. She turned her face into the wind and let her top eye wander. *Got to be some food around here, somewhere. Ain't giving up, Lord. But I could sure use some help.*

The once-promising breeze deposited windblown ash in the corners of her mouth and brought the gritty taste of ruin. If this was the answer to her prayer, maybe God didn't understand the question. She followed the breeze, anyway. Maybe God was white like in all the paintings or had a sense of humor beyond understanding.

Once a plantation, now an abandoned battlefield, piles of rubble marked where fireplaces once stood. The white picket fence around the perimeter had been hacked into pieces, and row upon row of simple white markers stretched the length of the property. Where tobacco once grew, graves sprouted.

Her footsteps slowed as she neared signs of the prison. White people might call it a plantation, but it was just another jail to the people enslaved here. The breeze died when she squatted behind a clump of smooth sumac and watched for trouble.

Why was it so quiet? Had all the people left? Maybe there was food.

A fancy road lined with massive oaks marked the formal entrance, but the path she cautiously followed led to the slave quarters, a worn strip of dirt along the bank of a foul-smelling creek full of garbage and sewage. A ten-foot tall, whitewashed wall once hid the unpleasant view of the slave quarters from the big house, but gaping holes were all that remained.

A decrepit shack was all that was left of a slave quarters too ramshackle to tear down, the sort of dilapidated hovels unfit for humans but reserved for the field slaves. "Doghouses," the house slaves called them, reserved for the lowest of the low: slaves who labored alongside the other animals. These one-room shanties, three big steps wide by four steps long, housed two or three families. The roofs leaked, dirt floors became mud in the rainy season, and Southern Kentucky's rainy season lasted most of the year. Daubing made from iron-rich clay soil filled the gaps. Red streaks formed on both sides of the walls when it rained. Peeling strips of bark from warped log walls gave the houses a tattered look and matched the clothes the slaves wore.

Rachel got down on her stomach and peered around the corner of an abandoned shack. If anybody was watching, they wouldn't think of looking for an intruder lying so close to the ground. She spied two elderly slaves who were too weak to travel and too old to sell, but if there were two people here, there could be others. She watched and waited. Decided to throw a rock against the side of their shack to see if anyone would rush to their aid. The rock thumped against the shack and dislodged a chunk of straw-filled plaster.

"Who's there?" An old woman, thin and slightly bent, the way a tree grows in rocky soil on a windy slope, peered through the door. "Hello?"

"Who is it, Mama?" This voice came from inside the shack.

"Shush," the old woman hissed.

Two people. Mother and daughter? Both of them probably too old to pose much of a threat. But was there anybody else?

Rachel waited until the old lady went back inside. She unwound her shawl and made a small bed for Samuel on the ground next to the wall where there was a strip of shade. She put her lips to his ear. You be a good boy and stay quiet."

"Dada?"

"Maybe later."

Samuel smiled and closed his eyes. He always got sleepy after nursing.

She kept low and peered around the corner, waited long enough to make certain nobody else was coming before she risked crossing the open space between the two shacks. She got down on her stomach and crawled up to the front door, risked a quick peek inside.

Her first glance confirmed the two elderly slaves were alone. Like many poor people in the South, they looked to be slowly starving to death. These women didn't seem like the answer to anybody's prayer. The oldest woman, the one who had peered through the door, still had some of her teeth; they gave her face a similar sense of resiliency that spoke of survival under harsh conditions. The other woman had sightless eyes, focused on something only she could see.

Rachel ducked back out of sight and retreated to the relative safety of the side of the shack. *They favor each other. Mother and daughter, probably. Got the same too-tough-to-die look. Don't look like they have food, but there must be water or they'd already be dead.*

She thumped the side of the shack with her fist to bring the mother back outside. This time, the old lady stepped onto the porch.

"Don't want to bring no trouble," she said, when the old woman peered around the corner.

"Then go away."

"Soon's I get some food."

"Everbody starvin'." The old woman shooed her away with a wave of her hand. "Don't need another mouth we can't feed."

"Not for me—for my baby. Or maybe just some water, I—"

"You running with a baby? Good Lord, child. Has you lost your mind?"

"Did you say baby?" A younger woman, hands held in front of her with the cautious movements of the blind, stepped onto the porch.

"Our people sold downriver," the old woman explained. "Massa gone back to England soon's fighting broke out."

"Both armies been through here." Her sightless eyes focused on an indistinct spot in the distance.

"Rebels ain't much for sharing," the old woman said.

"Been boiling leftover scraps, mostly. Tops and roots. Too thin to call soup," the daughter said, "but sitting at a table makes it seem like a meal."

"Be back soon's I get Samuel. He's so tired, probably won't wake up till tomorrow."

Rachel sat on a three-legged milking stool that rocked when she moved. A large oak stump served as a table and the bowls looked like they came from the same tree. A blackened pot hung above the fire. Yellowish-blue flames provided enough light to illuminate the humble surroundings, but there wasn't anything worth looking at. The soup wasn't much better: cast-off plant stems and leaves in warm water with a hint of flavor, but it was all the two women could find to eat and they shared it with her.

"Best meal I ate today," Rachel said.

A toothless grin spilt the ancient woman's face. "I 'spect a person could eat just about anything—call it tasty if they hungry enough."

"Yes, ma'am." Rachel returned the spoon to the pot while there was still enough broth left to start the next meal.

"There's water," the ancient woman said.

"Clean. And plenty of it," the other woman added.

"Here? The last river I crossed smelled like a chamber pot."

"There's a spring."

"Small, but steady."

"I can't see to find it—ain't seen nothing for so long, lost count of the years," the daughter said.

"And it's too far for me most days."

Now Rachel was certain they were mother and daughter. They favored each other in looks and seemed to share the same thoughts, took turns finishing each other's sentences.

"It hurt her to walk."

"And she can't see."

"But we getting by."

"Hard to believe anything survive," Rachel said. "Can't imagine this land ever coming back."

The grin on the daughter's face split wider. "We still here. More freedom in getting left to die than slaving."

The old woman nodded. "Look around. See these bare walls? We all alone here with nothing, but there's more hope around when there ain't nobody left to steal it."

"Been working this land all my life. Just cause I can't see don't mean I can't remember. Look out the door to your left..." The daughter listened for Rachel's footsteps before continuing. "See them trees? Full up with squirrels—enough of 'em to fill this stew pot ten times over.

Persimmons, too. Used to make pies and jam before I lost my sight."

"Even longer for me." The old woman's toothless smile meant it was a joke, not a complaint. "Look to your right—that's north. Find the path at the edge of that last fence and there's a buffalo trace that'll lead you to water."

"Know all about them bramble patches too mean for a plow," the daughter said. "They so thick neither army tangles with 'em. Every plantation in these parts has at least one patch so bad, there ain't no getting rid of it."

"And we both know where the water is and the armies ain't."

The old woman leaned closer. "Listen up. We'll tell you how to get free."

CHAPTER FOUR

Rachel crossed the southern end of the field where cannon had scorched the earth, then followed ruts carved into both sides of the riverbank at a shallow ford. Partway up the far shore she spotted a limestone outcropping. A jumbled pile of gray rocks lay beneath the eroded ledge, but a vibrant patch of green formed the landing. Water seeped from the lower third of the slope and a small artesian spring provided pure water in a land scarred by battle and fouled by death. Slowly but steadily, the spring refilled each tiny pool as she sipped the water directly from the smooth, hollowed-out rocks. She worked her way downhill and drained each pool with a couple of sips.

The water was cool, almost cold, and settled in her stomach with a comfortable heaviness. She drank her way to the bottom of the hill. There was a little more of a mineral taste toward the lower pools, but not enough to deter a thirsty woman.

Strange just sitting, not working. Ain't used to it. Maybe this is what it's like being white: no real work to do, nothing but sitting and waiting.

After she'd been still a while, the birds ignored her and resumed their conversations. She heard the scrape of claws digging into bark and looked up to see squirrels overhead. They jumped from branch to branch and leaped from tree to tree. The big, leafy, messy nests belonged to the squirrels. High up meant a hard winter.

It didn't take much to set up a squirrel pole: some rope and a stick big enough to lean against a tree. Squirrels could smell a trap if it was touched directly, so she removed the cord she used to hold up her skirt, covered her hands in mud, and moved away from the spring. She leaned the pole against a sweet gum tree with a nest among the top branches. She tied slipknots in each loop and wound the cord down the pole. The loops were muddy but the squirrels wouldn't mind. No matter which direction a squirrel climbed down the pole, eventually it was going to put its head through one of the loops. Squirrels were more curious than cautious, weren't smart enough to back out of a loop when it closed around their neck. Eventually they would get nervous, jump off the pole, and hang themselves. Curiosity would get the better of at least one squirrel, possibly two.

She went back to the spring and collected water. When she went back to the pole, two of the nooses were full. She reset the loops, then held up her skirt with one hand and returned to the shack.

"One for the pot and one for the roasting stick," she said, holding up two squirrels. "How's Samuel?"

"He ain't been no trouble," the daughter said. "Nice to have a little one around."

"Been taking turns," her mother said. "He keeps asking for his Daddy every time we switch."

"We both wishing he was here," Rachel said. The daughter couldn't see Rachel's tears and her mother was too polite to notice. They busied themselves with preparing the meal while Rachel nursed Samuel.

They shared the squirrel cooked over the fire while the one in the stew pot simmered.

"There's plenty more where these came from," Rachel said. "Can't run with one hand holding up my skirt, but I'll braid some cord and you won't go hungry."

"Rather starve free than eat another slave meal," the mother said.

"You ain't gonna starve," Rachel promised. "Squirrels too stupid for that."

"You ain't gonna have to run far. I promise," the daughter said. "Yankees is close. Rebels is closer."

"We kin tell you about both," her mother added. "Better, we kin show you the way past one and how to avoid the other."

Rachel laced enough nettles together to make squirrel traps and filled every container that would hold water. When the stew pot was full and the roasting fork held the next meal, the women guided her to a faint path that kept to the shadows.

"Slavers on the run," the daughter swore. "Union own the big rivers."

"You sure? No offense, ma'am, but ..."

"But what?"

"Well, are you certain the slavers are on the run?"

"You ever seen white man take a chance with his own life?" the mother asked.

"No, ma'am."

"That's why all them crackers around here is gone."

"And why they ain't been back since the Yankees come through," her daughter finished the sentence. "Follow this path, but keep your top eye open."

The path followed plantation boundaries and offered a tenuous connection between families separated by slavery. Husbands and wives, mothers and children once used this path to visit their loved ones. Four generations of footprints wore a path easily followed by moonlight. The women assured her it would lead to a stream she could follow to a river, but the path gave out and night passed without finding water.

Wish Joe was here, she thought when the night grew too quiet. *Wishing he was here for a whole lot of reasons and some I ain't thought of yet.*

While the early morning sky slowly changed to a translucent blue, but before the top of the sun cleared the horizon, she found a place to hide. A huge sycamore tree, the biggest one she'd ever seen, bore signs of a lightning strike. The trunk was hollow where the fire had burned its way down the branches and out one side. She drew a line in the direction the sun moved and placed a stick with the narrow end pointing from bottom to top. When she knew which way to run, she swept away the spider webs and crawled inside to sleep.

Grandma visited her in her dreams. Although the giant sycamore was but a hollow shell aboveground, its ancient roots reached deep into the earth where time remains connected to all things. Grandma bore every shade of green a healing plant might pass through. She let Rachel hear Joe find his courage. No burning bush or dramatic clap of thunder announced this decisive moment, but it was an epiphany all the same— one that formed a giant step along the freedom trail.

"Ain't no point standing in hell if I don't belong here," she heard Joe say. He half-whispered, half-mouthed, "Running my way into a new year; running toward Rachel and a new life worth living." He said the words the way a man would try on a pair of shoes. The words seemed to fit. *Was God putting words in his mouth, in his heart?*

⊷ ⊶

The wind blew life into the branches and they gently swayed in rhythmic appreciation. There was a community of animals who loved to talk, but these were the hunted, so their conversations were guarded. The haunting cry of a mourning dove tested the silence. A wolf risked voicing his displeasure at the rising moon. A corresponding howl from a distant hillside quieted the exploratory chatter of a raccoon family's foraging. Rachel's top eye warned her that she wasn't alone.

She waited for the acrid smell of smoke from a cigarette, watched for the soft red glow from a lit pipe or cigar, listened for the heavy breathing of a bounty hunter who wasn't used to sitting still. Sometimes their horses gave them away. Horses were worse at staying quiet than any man.

She searched in an ever-widening circle until two small clumps of matted grass told her where two escaped slaves had spent the night. The pungent odor of filthy clothing overpowered the smell of decaying leaves, but nothing smelled stronger than fear. She followed a faint trail of bent and broken grass blades that led toward an animal trail skirting the hilltops.

Oaks, maples, pine and beech trees shielded her from bounty hunters and the local, slave-owning populace. She came to a stream and found two sets of footprints at a spot shallow enough to wade across, then followed the stream until it became a river. Where another river joined it, there was a farm nestled among the fertile lowlands. She unwound her shawl and took Samuel off her back, then crouched on one knee beside an evergreen tree and let her top eye tell her if it was safe.

A smoke plume drifted away from the chimney and reformed as a cloudbank beneath the cold air at the top of the valley. She waited while the logs inside the fireplace became embers. The hardwood trees beside her creaked as the temperature settled below freezing.

I don't mind the cold, long as it's keeping bounty hunters inside.

A gentle breeze swirled around the hills and twist-ed the smoke into ethereal shapes. *That one looks a little like Grandma. Funny how I feel her watching over me.*

Her brief smile at the memory dissipated along with the familiar shape. *She seems so close-by, I wonder if I'll ever stop missing the people I lost?*

A winterberry shrub offered protection from watchful eyes. She crept closer to the house and peered through the bright red berries. The house bore outward signs of neglect, but rusty hinges swung on oiled inner workings. Sun-bleached posts belied their hardwood origins. It looked like the home of a prosperous free black man. Woe unto a black man who advertised his success, for jealous whites would sooner sabotage a black man's gains than work toward their own.

She allowed herself a faint smile of relief—the first since she couldn't remember when. This was the house of a man willing to look the other way. The aroma of home cooking drifted downwind. It was make-do cooking: turnip and collard greens, with the barest hint of fatback, but with the aromas of a cook who knew how to turn cast-off food into savory fare. It was poor people's food; cheap but tasty. It should be safe. She approached the house and knocked twice on the door and once on the wall next to it.

"Don't want to bring no trouble," she whispered.

Someone eased the door open a crack, but remained hidden inside. "Is you alone?"

"Yes. Just me and my baby—Samuel."

The door opened a few more inches and an arm reached out to hurry her inside. A black man, stocky and wearing bib overalls shook his head in dismay. His wife huddled in the corner with her arms around two small children.

"Seen Rebel scouts for five days now," he said. "Bounty hunter been by last night, too. That men mean a whole lot a trouble. More'n I can stand. Got two more like you hid in the barn."

"Seen their footprints and followed them," Rachel said. "It's how I found you."

His wife gasped. "You got to go," she said.

"She's right. Sorry," the farmer hooked his thumbs on the straps of his overalls. "You best take them two hiding in the barn with you."

"Manger good enough for God's son," his wife added, "but that won't stop no bounty hunter from burning down our barn."

"I'll hitch up the mules and we'll take my wagon. I can get you to the far side of town. After that, well— let's just say it's best if you don't even know my name."

"And take the little ones," his wife grabbed his arm. "They over the pox but the sores is still showing."

"After that, you on your own," the farmer said.

Rachel nodded. "Been on my own most my life."

CHAPTER FIVE

Before the morning breeze blew away their cover, Rachel and the farmer crept to the uphill side of the barn. If the moon should peek from behind the clouds and cast their shadows against the barn, they would be low and indistinct. A gentle rush of warm, hay-scented air flowed past when the farmer opened the door wide enough to squeeze inside. A mule whinnied. Her nose told her the stalls needed to be mucked out.

"Hercules," he whispered. "Aveta."

"Afraid you wasn't coming."

Rachel jumped at the low whisper, but relaxed when a young girl crawled out from beneath a mound of hay and brushed the remaining strands off her clothes. Petite, with dark, flawless skin: the first blush of womanhood was visible on her face. She was a beautiful child, but a beautiful daughter was a curse to a slave family. Her thick eyebrows formed a quizzical "v" as she peered at Rachel.

"C'mon on, Hercules," she whispered.

A hand and part of a muscular arm emerged from beneath the hay. When she grasped the hand and pulled, a six-foot-tall mound of hay cascaded to the floor. The man bore a close likeness to a scarecrow. Straw clung to his hair and jutted from beneath his sleeves. "Who this?" He stared at Rachel.

An "R," for "runaway," had been branded onto his left cheek from a recent escape attempt. Blisters dotted the unhealed edges of the scar, bright pink against his coal black skin.

"The answer to your prayers," the farmer said. "You got to go before that bounty hunter come back. Now get in the wagon and keep quiet." He set a lantern next to his wagon and lowered the flame until it sputtered, then twisted the wick up a degree until the light steadied. "Melons is best for hiding under, but corncobs, oats and hay the best I can do on short notice."

Rachel helped the farmer remove the tarp covering his wagon and they spread it on the ground. The wagon would be unloaded several times, and muddy cargo made bounty hunters and pattyrollers suspicious. Joe had told her about patrollers, or "pattyrollers," people who watched the roads and rivers for escaped slaves. The reward for returning an escaped slave was more money than most people made in two years from honest work.

Corncobs wouldn't support boards the way melons could, so the runaways would be uncomfortable, but with a thick layer of hay and oats on top, they would be hidden. The farmer transported anything he could resell, so his wagon was a familiar sight. If his cargo remained quiet and their luck held, maybe they wouldn't be spotted.

"Lay on your side." He didn't give them enough time to get nervous and used a tone of voice that discouraged questions. "Tuck your arms under your face, Hercules. Leave some space for your head, Aveta. Both of you, cup your hands over your mouth and make a little hollow for air to seep through. Breathe in slow an' easy."

He placed a small board on each side of Hercules' head, then rested sacks of feed corn against them so they wouldn't move. He placed another board on top and created a three-sided box around Hercules' head so he could breathe. Pumpkins, melons, potatoes, or sacks of feed corn, anything would hide a person willing to be uncomfortable. With a mound of hay on top, no one would think of looking for an escaped slave beneath so much cargo—Rachel hoped.

Hercules moaned. Hearing him, Aveta shied away from the wagon and looked ready to run in the opposite direction.

"Can't breathe!" Hercules moaned a little louder. "Feel the Devil walking across my grave."

"Hush up. You got to stay quiet," the farmer said. "And quit shaking. You gonna spook the mules." He helped Aveta into the wagon and gently rolled her onto her side, showed her how to keep her arms around her face so she would be able to breathe.

"Walls is closing in," Hercules moaned. "Squeezing me too tight to breathe."

"Then bite down on your finger or something. You got to stay quiet." The farmer helped Rachel climb into the back of the wagon. "Raise your knees toward your chest, so's you can make room for the baby."

Rachel cradled Samuel against her chest so he would have a safe place to rest and could nurse if he got hungry. She settled onto her side next to Hercules, felt him shaking and reached out to comfort him.

He recoiled from her touch. "Devil reaching for my soul."

"It's me, Hercules," Rachel whispered. "Close your eyes. Think about staying quiet."

"Thought you was Satan. God help me. Ain't long for this world."

"Quiet," Aveta whispered. "Scoot closer to me if that'll help."

"Spent six long weeks chained in a slaver," Hercules pulled his knees together and hunched his shoulders inward. He crossed his legs at the ankles so their bodies weren't touching. "Can't stand nobody touching me, neither."

"Close your eyes and take deep breaths. Concentrate on staying quiet."

"Less worse, maybe," he whispered. "Ain't no better."

The corncobs were in sacks and she could hear the boards groan under the combined weight as the farmer stacked a layer of sacks above them. She kept one hand on Samuel's head to protect him and cupped the other one around her face so she wouldn't be smothered from the inevitable dust that shook loose from the hay and oats. A layer of dirt formed on the boards around her. The sacks were damp, the oats and straw dusty. The bile rose in her throat. *Oh Lord, little Samuel can't breathe! The dogs is coming.* She opened her eyes to prove to herself she wasn't underwater. *Breathe,* she reminded herself. *Shallow breaths. Remember where you are.*

Hercules coughed. Aveta sneezed. Samuel started crying.

"Help!" Hercules used his elbows to push the sacks of corn aside. He grabbed the edge of the wagon and pulled his head above the oats and corn. "Couldn't get no air. Felt like I was drownin' in a pile of dust."

Rachel slid from beneath the oats and hay covering the bags of feed corn. "Maybe if we put some more boards down, give us a little room to breathe."

"Risk getting caught you do that," the farmer pointed out.

"Get caught for sure with all this carrying on," Rachel said. "Passion root would settle everybody down, but I'm all out."

"Couple sips of moonshine ought to do it. Got a jar hidden away in the corner." The farmer grinned sheepishly. "My wife don't like it."

"Scared of tight spaces." Hercules climbed out of the wagon and bowed his head. "Sorry. Felt Satan grabbing aholt of my soul!"

Rachel fed a couple of sips of moonshine to Samuel. Aveta and Hercules took a few gulps for courage. Once again they crawled onto the floor of the wagon. Sacks of feed corn, bags of oats and mounds of hay hid them from view and gave the illusion of a full load.

The farmer gently placed his children near the side of the wagon so they wouldn't be sitting directly on top of the runaways. They were past the contagious stage but bore signs of the pox on their faces. He took his place in the driver's seat. "Pull. Get on there."

Rachel smiled at hearing this; most freed slaves refused to own a whip.

"C'mon now, pull." The mules pulled and the wagon lumbered forward. Once it was under way, they settled into a comfortable pace. There was a soothing effect to the rhythmic creak and gentle swaying of the wagon, similar to rocking in a cradle if she could ignore sacks of feed corn and a couple hundred pounds of hay and oats balanced on top of her head. Hercules moaned maybe once or twice, at times she swore she could hear Aveta praying, but little Samuel stayed quiet. She added a silent prayer of her own. *Thank you, Lord.*

The wagon shuddered to a stop. She heard foot-steps. It was hard to figure out what was happening without being able to see anything, but the number of steps sounded about right for someone to walk from a tollbooth to the wagon.

"What the hell you got back here?" a man with a baritone voice yelled. Rachel felt the sacks of corn above her head move when he pushed them aside for a closer look. He must have been holding a torch be-cause she smelled burning tar. She felt cold steel graze her leg and heard a "thunk" when he stabbed a pitch-fork through the hay. She felt the wagon shudder when he yanked the tines out of the wood. She held her breath, prayed for the next thrust to miss her, but God wasn't listening. This "thunk" wasn't as loud—fewer tines having lodged in the wooden floor because two of them were imbedded in her leg. She tensed every muscle in her body to not scream from the pain.

It hurt worse when the pattyroller ripped the tines out of her leg. *Thank God he missed Samuel.*

The pitchfork came slashing downward a third time. Hercules remained silent, but she felt the muscles in his back contract. He didn't utter a sound. The next stab must have brought the pattyroller close enough to the children for a better look at their sores.

"What the h—? Is that the pox? Git them children the hell outa here!"

The wagon creaked as they started moving. She could hear the pattyroller cursing at the farmer for not leaving faster.

The gradual slowing of hoof beats and a change in the wagon's angle told her the mules were struggling up a hill. She heard the mules strain as the wagon left the road's smooth surface, and then felt the wagon bounce over rough terrain for long enough to be well off the road. One of the children jumped off the wagon; Rachel felt the weight of corn and hay resting on her head lighten by about sixty pounds.

"Up you go." The load lightened accordingly as the farmer helped his second child off the mound of hay and oats. "Go lie on your stomach underneath the branches and watch the road."

Rachel heard the swish of a child running through grass.

The tarp rustled with each loosened knot. Armfuls of hay being removed left behind dust but didn't reduce the weight pressing down on top of her by much. The wagon rocked with each unloaded sack of corn.

It got easier to breathe. She heard bags of oats being tossed to the ground; the sound reminded her of someone fluffing up a tick, and she pictured the puff of air whooshing out of the burlap sacks each time they yielded to a callused palm.

Strong hands grabbed her ankles and tugged her from beneath the hay. She was the first to be pulled from the wagon and recognized the farmer by his battered hat. She looked at the sky. Dawn was near, and a storm was brewing; thick clouds scuttled by the weak moon. Her eyes adjusted to the faint light, but the farmer remained a shadowy form silhouetted against the evening sky.

Maybe it's better this way. Not knowing names or seeing faces is a good way to keep from being turned in for reward money.

She strapped Samuel to her back to free both hands. She took her place beside the farmer and formed a human chain unloading the wagon. They uncovered Hercules next. Blood stained his pants where the pitchfork had punctured his leg.

"I's alright," he said. "How about you, Miss Rachel?"

"Pain's just a part of getting free." Together they helped Aveta from beneath the last sacks of corn.

Rachel, Hercules and Aveta formed another human chain and helped reload the wagon. The hay went back on top, fluffed up so it would look the same as when the farmer first set out. The children clambered aboard. The mules pulled. The wagon lumbered back onto the road, under way before anyone was likely to notice the brief stop. With luck, the coming rain would erase all signs of the detour. As the steady clip-clop of mule hooves faded into the distance, Rachel led them deeper into the forest.

CHAPTER SIX

Bo Magruder hammered a runaway slave notice to the message post with a rusty nail. If the wind had been blowing the opposite way, Rachel would have heard the sound of the hammer striking metal. She was hiding on the outskirts of Perryville, Kentucky. Bo was less than a mile away, standing on the sidewalk of the small town's main street. The freckles splattered across his forehead matched his flushed cheeks. A knife scar gave him a squinty eye and bisected the middle of his lower lip. His crooked nose leaned toward the left side of his face. The hammer glanced off the nail and struck his thumb.

"Goddamnit-all-to-hell," he muttered, running the words together to act as a springboard for more cursing. A bounty hunter and war profiteer, Bo Magruder began working both sides as soon as the Confederates opened fire on Fort Sumter. He stuck his thumb in his mouth to ease the pain and stepped away from the notice:

> Reward offered, for information leading to the capture of a young slave woman. Answers to the name of Rachel. Dark complexion with a small curved scar over left eye. Wearing brown calico dress, between 16 and 18 years of age, 5-feet-1-or-2 inches of height, with infant, pleasant countenance, curly hair, large breasts and slender build.

The reward for information was enough money to tempt an abolitionist's conscience: 200 dollars, enough to buy a working farm with fertile soil. Bo could afford to be generous; the reward for Rachel's return was more money than most people made in five years. Bo studied the other notices. He wasn't much for reading and could barely write more than enough to sign his name, but a bounty hunter didn't need book learning.

Rachel closed her eyes, willed herself to remain calm. The Union Army might have control of the city, but the citizens of Perryville still owned slaves. *Maybe God will help. Give me that top eye,* she prayed, *and while You're at it, if You're listening, help Joe, too. You the only one he got left. Help him get free and watch over him as soon as he's on his way. Amen.*

She listened for an answer to her prayers.

Nothing. Maybe the answer was "no." Or maybe the answer was "not yet."

An answer to her prayers came in degrees. The solution eased up on her when she was all the way settled down. Staying close to the road felt like a trap, so she did what most escaped slaves do: kept moving and stayed out of sight.

"C'mon," she whispered. "We got to go before that bounty hunter catches up." She showed Aveta and Hercules how to slide their feet under the fallen leaves and avoid trampling the grass. "Stay quiet, stay alive."

They hid behind oak trees that refused to let go of last year's dead leaves, passed beneath ghostly white sycamore branches, sidestepped tulip poplars and sweet gum trees. The last tree big enough to hide behind was a shagbark hickory at the edge of an abandoned battlefield. A shroud of loss and loneliness lay draped upon the ruined earth. The wind shifted and brought the stench of rotting carcasses. She covered her nose and mouth with her sleeve, motioned for Aveta and Hercules to do the same. A barren swath of land led toward the river. Fallen horses clogged the ruined streambed, and a dam had formed where a fetid trash mound surrounded their corpses. She hurriedly traversed a fallen tree until it was no longer possible to keep it from spinning and risked a rolling jump to the far shore.

Aveta crossed without incident. Hercules went last. He waited until the log steadied, waved his arms for balance, but the makeshift log bridge started spinning before he was halfway across. His last step was into the greenish-black froth covering shallow water.

"Shit!" One shoe squelched and oozed pond scum as he limped away from the riverbank.

"Sshh. Quiet."

A dense briar patch flourished at the far edge of the battlefield. A large ashen clearing offered a recessed hiding place in the patch, with enough space to burrow out of sight.

"Samuel's getting hungry," Rachel whispered. "Got to clean him up some, too. Hercules, Aveta, put your backs together so's you can be sure and watch both ways."

About the time they got settled in, an unsaddled horse limped into view through the thorns. Its uneven gait and unbalanced half steps gave it the appearance of being lame, but as it moved closer, she could see it was hobbled with a leather strap between its two front legs.

The horse nudged aside the thorny bushes where small patches of grass remained beneath the brambles. Its bridle rattled against the sheltering thicket, the metallic clink unnaturally loud in a forest sparsely populated by nocturnal hunters. She didn't see the horse's owner until a brief flare of light formed a halo above his head. The tip of his cigarette glowed with enough light to reveal his unshaven face and wool jacket: the bounty hunter.

Run! Or hide? Top eye, where you at? Got to be some way outta here.

There's a difference between looking and seeing, Grandma reminded her.

Rachel stared at the terrain long enough to see the little things most people missed.

Another memory came to her, something she'd heard on a rainy Sunday during story time. Rachel leaned over until her lips touched Hercules' ear. "Get ready. Pain coming."

Hercules looked at the thorns, then at his bare hands. He hunched his shoulders forward. He grabbed the loose ends of his sleeves with his hands to use as makeshift mittens.

Aveta nodded and followed his example.

Rachel removed Samuel from her back and used her shawl to bind him to her chest. She held her forearms in front of Samuel so he wouldn't get hurt. He didn't like not being able to see but she had to protect him from the thorns. Thorns poked through her sleeves and punctured her skin. She clenched her jaw against the pain, pushed aside the branches, and fought her way into the thicket.

They eased deeper into the brambles and brushed aside leaf litter that might betray their stealthy movements. A mass of tangled thorns big enough to detour an army would allow them to pass through, if they were willing to endure pain. The barbs pierced her flesh, but she steeled herself to the sting. Aveta eased in behind her. Hercules followed.

Inch by inch, thorn prick by thorn prick, they reached the other side. The sunbonnet had kept Rachel's hair from snagging in the thorns, but her dress was dotted with fresh blood and her arms looked like she had been mauled by a lion. Gently, she pulled the thorns out of her skin. The ends of Hercules' sleeves were tattered, his hands covered with blood. Aveta silently wept.

The land was plowed under with the promise of winter wheat yet to reveal itself beyond a few small patches of light green. Rachel crouched close to the ground and took one careful step at a time. *Give me strength, Lord,* she prayed. *Maybe add some courage.* She waited for her top eye to tell her if it was safe.

Nothing. Ain't no cigar smoke or noisy horses. She kept her eyes closed so she could focus on listening. *Still nothing.*

When she was all listened out, she opened her eyes. Silently, she thanked Grandma who taught her the secret to having a top eye—that a "top eye" saw what was missing. Birds were better than watchdogs at sensing intruders. If she settled in and waited, and remained perfectly still, eventually the birds would accept her presence and return to foraging—unless someone else was nearby. *Maybe trouble comes in groups of two if you're a bird,* she thought. If someone else was already in the area, the birds wouldn't leave the trees no matter how long she waited. She knew it was safe to move when a blue jay swooped to the ground in search of seeds.

The night became a series of cautious advances. Bounty hunters shot at anyone who moved and citizens looking for reward money hunted whomever they missed. Craters pockmarked the fields on either side of her, but the Devil owned the stretch of road cutting through the center. Uprooted tree stumps sprawled upside down, their crooked roots reached to the sky with skeletal fingers. Gnarled branches cast eerie shadows on the scorched earth.

"Smells like we're close to a swamp," Rachel said. "From now on, step where I step and slide your feet. Bounty hunters set rope traps in swamps. You got to cut yourself out of a rope trap and I ain't got no knife. If you fall into a bounty hunter's pit, ain't no climbing out."

Give me that top eye, Lord. Sure need it now.

She waited until she could be certain there was no one nearby, then led Hercules and Aveta away from the forest. They crossed a muddy field. To stand for too long in one place meant slowly settling toward an indefinite bottom. The next bog held a special kind of mud: a sticky, clumpy morass that clung to the bottom of her feet. The farther she walked, the taller she got. When pieces of trash starting showing up, it meant an army camp was nearby.

"I recognize this place," Rachel said. "We still near Perryville, might be as far north as Harrodsburg. Ain't sure, but I know there ain't nothing but slave traders and Confederate sympathizers around here." She broke the bad news as gently as she could. "Means we got to keep to the river, maybe steal us a boat—if we get lucky."

"Is that safe?" Aveta asked.

"Nothing's safe."

"Why a boat?" Hercules shook his head and sighed. "What's wrong with taking another road?"

"Ain't that many roads. Don't take much money to hire enough people to watch every route."

"Why can't we just sneak past?" Aveta asked.

"Dawgs. I didn't hear none. Don't mean that bounty hunter won't get some."

Hercules gave both of them a worried look. "I hates being wet. I hates boats worse, but I hates dawgs worst of all."

"C'mon. We got to keep quiet." Rachel turned toward the northwest. "Each footstep's about life or death: a free life, or the slow death of being a slave."

CHAPTER SEVEN

Aclump of red cedar trees offered rudimentary shelter. An artesian spring, dormant during the winter season, formed a hollow in the center of the small forest, and the skeleton of a fiddlehead fern lay at the base of the largest seep. Darkened streaks on a limestone outcropping hinted at occasional water that percolated through fissures during the wet season. The promise of spring was a long way off, but the threat of daylight was here. Rachel chose a large stick and pointed it toward the North. She unwrapped Samuel from her back, cleaned and nursed him, then gently rocked him to sleep. She formed a soft crib out of pine needles and covered him with her shawl and a blanket of leaves.

She shook Aveta's shoulder to wake her and helped her climb under a low limestone ledge. The small ledge formed a windbreak and provided a narrow strip of dry ground, while the south-facing orientation held promise of warmth. Aveta curled up close to the cliff face and fashioned a crude pillow from the windblown sand.

"Hid in worse places." Hercules helped gather branches to build a skimpy wall around Aveta. It was a crude blanket but would help keep her warm and hide her from view.

Rachel carried the leftover pile of branches to another small outcropping nearby. "You're next."

"What about you?" Hercules yawned wide enough for Rachel to see a gap in his back teeth.

"I'll take the first watch so you can rest up."

"I kin build a fire. The kind that don't smoke much. Won't give off hardly no light but make plenty of heat."

"Maybe later." She piled the leftover branches around him, and then moved away from the cliff to where Virginia creeper twirled around the trunk of a large white oak. She stripped the leaves from the vines and laced the tough strands together to form a thin cord. This she strung between two trees, placed high enough for a horse to pass beneath but low enough to sweep a bounty hunter out of the saddle.

Samuel was asleep, so she leaned against a black rock and turned toward the southeast so the sun would warm her. There was nothing to do but wait for the return of darkness and the slight protection it offered from the bounty hunter who refused to leave them alone.

Her intention to stay awake was no match for lack of sleep and a comfortable spot in the sun's warmth. No amount of resolve or discipline was stronger than fatigue, and dreams seldom came but nightmares rarely stayed away for long. No slave knew peace, for slavery was a nightmare, and her sixteen years of slavery had seemed endless when one minute, one second, was an eternity. Those miserable days refused to remain buried. She fought off sleep but she couldn't stay awake forever. The nightmares returned...

This particular nightmare dragged her back to that awful day she learned of Grandma's death. The bad news reached her at the end of a long day spent stringing tobacco. The sweltering heat made distant objects shimmer the way they did underwater. The nicotine from the leaves left her weak and dizzy. She was short of breath. A throbbing headache made it painful to blink. She was too tired to cook but her stomach hurt too much to go hungry, and just when she thought it couldn't get any worse, Old Shaky came pounding on her door.

"Git yore lazy ass over to the Reynold's place." Old Shaky's whip hand quivered. "They got some sick nigger they want you to look after."

Old man Reynold had outlived his youngest son and was too mean to die. He used a box to walk out to the fields, pushing it a few inches in front of his feet, and then shuffling along behind. He leaned on the box and yelled at his slaves as they worked the fields.

Good Lord. Reynold's place is eight miles away. But... she hid her smile from Old Shaky. *This means I'll see Grandma twice this month. I know every step to the Reynold's place from all those trips during the Promise Moon. Wonder if Grandma ever felt this tired when she was coming the other way to see me?*

Rachel cut across the Boone Plantation where the mulatto slave children had curly blond hair, but took the long way around the Jones Plantation to avoid the vicious hounds. It was a three hour walk to the Reynold's Plantation, but she'd made the trip in two-and-a-half hours on the Promise Moon when it meant spending more time with Grandma.

A new split rail fence lined the wide road leading toward the Reynold's house. The quartered logs still had green centers. Aromatic, dark-red cedar wood countered the stench from the sewage ditch leading toward the slave village.

Sounds like I'm already too late. Rachel heard wailing. *Walked all this way for nothing and now I got to turn right around and walk back. Started out tired and it ain't ever gonna get no better,'cept it can't get no worse.*

But it can always get worse. Rachel clutched Grandma's cold hand.

Now I understand why the women are wailing. If only I hadn't dawdled. I could—no, should have been with her when she passed to the other side.

Grief tore a hole in Rachel's soul. She cried until her sorrow grew deep enough to wail. Her voice turned hoarse when she screamed from the hurt. When nothing was left—not even hope, she laid her head on Grandma's cold body and wished to join her.

Grandma eased into Rachel's dream from the other side. She took her by the hand and led her away from her slaving days to a smooth road where "The North" was more than a promise.

Grandma was free, her beautiful soul had shed a slave's living hell and no whip could touch her. Grandma used the zigzag shape of light filtering through the trees to angle Rachel's dream away from an open-air prison of plantation life. She hovered on the edge of her consciousness, where a top eye could see a little bit into the future.

Your life's path ain't straight, child. Only God can see where you're gonna end up, but he's letting me take a peek. Don't you worry. I seen enough to know you gonna be all right. You always were. That ain't gonna change. Look over there. She pointed toward a familiar figure standing by the edge of a battlefield. *Recognize him? That's Joe. I'm watching over him. He's stealing himself free.*

Little Samuel wailed with the urgency of a hungry baby in a soiled diaper. Rachel tried to sit up and bumped her head against the limestone outcropping sheltering Aveta. When she raised her hand to rub the bump, her elbow collapsed the crude shelter of branches and twigs. The clatter snapped Hercules awake, and he had the presence of mind to keep his head down but hit his shoulder on the wooden barrier and sent it crashing against a nearby winterberry shrub.

Oh no! Rachel snapped awake. *I slept all day.*

Aveta screamed.

All we need is a lumberjack yelling 'Timber!' to make this noise complete. Can't get no worse.

A dog howled.

Guess I was wrong. "C'mon," Rachel hissed. "We got to risk the water."

"What?" Hercules grabbed her arm. "Spent six weeks on the Ohio River. Locked in the hold of a slave ship and chained to a dead man for most of it. Ain't there nothing else?"

"The slow death," Rachel said. "Going back to being a slave."

"Then why we waiting?" Aveta grabbed a stick to use as a club.

"Follow me." Rachel dropped to her knees and motioned for them to do the same. She heard a horse whinny and nearly lost her courage when she looked toward the road; the bounty hunter's silhouette was visible from the torch he held over his head. He was so close, she could see the freckles on his face and the flames matched the color of his hair. The torch flickered in the wind but didn't go out when spurred his horse toward them.

"What is it?" Aveta whispered. "What's wrong?"

Rachel shook her head. "This way. Quick! Bounty hunter just up the road. He'll be here before we can reach the forest."

"That ain't but a minute or two away if we running. What if he seen us?" Hercules asked.

"Ain't waiting around to find out." Rachel led them to a steep hill above the river. Rocky soil crumbled underfoot with their first steps down the steep slope, but gnarled tree roots offered occasional footholds. A stand of firs clinging to the hill sheltered them from the bounty hunter, but the hounds could smell them. Rachel pulled her shawl tight against her chest to keep Samuel from slipping off her back and held on to the branches with both hands. A couple of her fingers were stuck together with pinesap by the time they neared the river. When the ground leveled out and there were no more trees to offer shelter, the wind began splattering her with raindrops.

"Help me look for a boat."

"Can't see nothin'," Hercules said.

"Looks like something over there. Think I see some boats." Rachel pointed toward a pier partially obscured by low-hanging clouds.

"You must be part owl," Aveta said. "I don't see nothing."

Rachel didn't like boats. She could swim, though. Joe had taught her. But she didn't have his love of the water. "Clouds is about to let loose," she said. "Maybe the rain will hide us."

"Lawd help me," Hercules moaned. "Here I been thinking it can't get no worse."

They found a small boat with a big leak. Water collected in the bottom as they pushed away from shore. Rachel sat in front and bailed. Aveta sat on the edge of the stern behind Hercules. Samuel cried.

"Marse Speed should of named me Poseidon instead of Hercules." He threaded the oars through their locks. "Years of swamp work, and I hates being wet worst of all."

"At least the storm's helping us stay hid. The clouds are blocking the moon, keeping it too dark to see," Rachel said. "Quickest way north is on the water." The wind scattered her words. The little wooden boat creaked and groaned. Samuel became seasick and vomited on Hercules' back. The wind splattered partially digested and sour-smelling milk on all of them. Rachel bailed water and Hercules pulled harder on the oars.

"I'se not wearing chains," he muttered. He rowed to the rhythm of his words. "I ain't," he whispered as he raised the oars and moved them forward, "chained to no dead man." He used his legs to help pull on the oars.

Rachel heard Aveta praying. A gust of wind carried the words, "God" and "please."

"I'se not," a wave splashed over the side, "in no slave ship," Hercules whispered. "And if I get to Canady," he pulled on the oars, "buying land as far from water as I can get." He moved the oars swiftly forward. "Moving so far from water," he closed his eyes, "won't never see no more except to drink." He pulled on the oars. "Lord help me." He whispered these last words to save his breath for rowing.

Rachel noticed the wind pushing the boat backward before he could return the oars to the water. He saw her watching and nodded. "Longer I'se rowing, less we're going."

She peered through the rain. "Can't see much, but the water looks calmer over there. Row that way, maybe it's a cove. We take on any more water, we'll be swimming 'stead of floating."

"Where?" Hercules stopped mid-stroke. "Which way? Still can't see a thing."

"To your left," she pointed toward an irregular patch of gray, slightly darker than the water. "Hear the waves?"

"Sounds like they hitting rocks." He pulled on one oar to keep the boat steady.

"Not rocks. Trees...I hope."

The trees were bare, but the overhanging branches offered an anchor. She grasped a limb and pulled the boat next to shore. "We'll wait here."

"We getting out?" he asked. "Standing on land's better than sitting in water."

"We'll wait for the wind to die down some." The wind blew through her wet clothes and didn't stop until it reached her bones. She cradled Samuel against her chest and turned her back toward the wind. Turning numb eased the pain somewhat but didn't stop her teeth from chattering. She clenched her mouth shut, and when that didn't work any longer, she lowered her head and bit down on her dress. She endured. They would be free. Samuel, all cried out, gave a miserable-sounding whimper. Rachel pressed her arms against her sides and huddled over Samuel to block as much of the wind as she could.

"Think the wind's dying down some." Aveta licked her finger, held it up to the wind. It was mostly from habit. It was still raining.

"Think I feel it slacking off some, too," Hercules said. "You was right moving back to land. Probably be more right moving all the way in till we standing on dirt."

"Ain't safe. Daylight's coming," Rachel pointed east. "See it in the clouds?" The lower edge of the horizon showed a faint tint of opaque red.

"Got to be a place to hide on land," Hercules said, squinting into the fog.

"Not for long. Nothing but bounty hunters and pattyrollers living here. We either move or get caught. We'll stay in the boat and keep close to shore. Wind slackens off a little in the shallows." She shivered, but not because of the cold. "That bounty hunter is still out there somewhere—close. I can feel it."

"Don't want no more'a that bounty hunter." Hercules slipped the oars into the water and leaned forward until Rachel could feel the buttons on his shirt. "I ain't," the familiar cadence helped get the last little bit of distance from each stroke, "getting caught."

Rachel and Aveta bailed. Hercules rowed. They endured. When it seemed unbearable, when they were as wet as they could get, and too cold to feel, when there was no hope left, the rain slacked off.

"Believe the rain ain't blowing sideways no more." Hercules turned his face into the wind.

A gust of wind blew the rain from the opposite direction. The next few gusts peppered them with hail before the storm left them alone.

"Think the storm is moving south." Rachel twisted around so she could study the southern sky. "Looks like the storm's breaking up behind us."

"Hoping it takes this wind with it," Aveta said.

Rachel watched the squall roll across the river valley. The wind began to blow their clothes dry instead of driving rain through to the skin. Each gust moved the clouds farther apart until she could look up and be comforted by a view of the heavens. It was a waning moon, and her old friend the Drinking Gourd was bright in the northern sky. White people called it the Big Dipper and entertained their children with tales of ancient heroes, but to her, it pointed the way toward freedom. Grandma taught her about the stars.

Maybe she's up there watching over me. Sure feels like it. Hear her whistling when the wind's just right. Feel her arms wrap around me when a good dream visits.

Hercules rowed until his arms ached. Rachel and Aveta bailed water until their hands turned so cold they couldn't feel their fingers. The wind died down but refused to leave. Each gust pushed the boat backward when Hercules brought the oars forward.

"Ain't no use," Rachel said. "We got to get off the water. Getting too close to daylight to be out here much longer."

"Don't see nothing but rocks and open space," Aveta said. "How we gonna hide in all that?"

"Ain't nothing else. This way, Hercules." Rachel pointed to her right. "Turn around some. Headin' downwind the only way we'll make it to shore." She unwrapped her shawl and gently handed Samuel to Aveta. "Try and keep him out of the wind." She jumped out of the boat, but the water was over her head, and she swallowed a mouthful of the river. She hung on to the side of the boat and coughed the water out of her lungs, caught her breath, and then ducked below the surface to push the boat from behind. Hercules laid down the oars and jumped overboard to help. Together, they pushed the boat far enough ashore so the current wouldn't drag it back in. "Get out of the boat, Aveta." Rachel pointed toward an opening behind a grove of trees to the north. "We'll drag it over there and keep moving."

The wind was at her back and Grandma passed over from the other side to let her glimpse through the veil separating the living from the unknown. Rachel peered past the last tendrils of fog at the edge of the clearing and the answer became apparent as the last vestiges of mist drifted from view.

"C'mon Hercules. Aveta, we got to keep moving. We need somebody to die."

"What?" Hercules asked. Aveta cowered.

"What we need is a funeral," Rachel said. "Follow me and I'll explain."

CHAPTER EIGHT

Scraggly chokecherry bushes and bayberry shrubs grew along the forest edge. Hercules stood guard and watched for trouble. Rachel left Samuel in Aveta's care and followed a path of steady decline leading toward the area of Lawrenceburg, Kentucky where blacks were allowed. No one stopped her because she made sure no one saw her.

The African Methodist Episcopalian church was small, square and unassuming, a simple building with one window on each side. The dormant trees were trimmed and looked ready for spring. An older man, slightly bent with age, emerged from the basement door, which must be where his quarters were. Two tufts of gray hair sheltered his ears but the rest of his head shone shiny and black in the sunlight.

He went inside the main building; in a few minutes, a thick smoke plume announced the promise of a warm interior. The church bell moved next. The clapper's first strike rang off-key, but as the bell began to swing, a pure tone called the faithful to worship. A few minutes later, the caretaker disappeared through the basement door.

A bloodhound's howl worked its way downhill and echoed off the building. Bloodlust colored their excited wails. The dogs knew she was here.

With little time for caution, she crossed the open space, raised her hand and knocked twice on the basement door, then once on the wall beside it.

The caretaker eased open the door to his quarters. "Why you comin' round here in daylight?" he whispered.

"You my last chance." It was close enough to begging to hurt her pride.

"Come inside 'fore someone sees you."

"Can't. Got to keep moving. Just need a funeral."

"You ain't gettin' far lookin' like that. Your eyes is sunk back in your head. And your clothes? Ain't nobody mistaking you for nuthin' but a runaway. Lawd, child." He wrinkled his nose in distaste. "You been swimming in the river out by the sewage dump? We got to git you cleaned up and wearin' somethin' decent."

"No time—now, about that funeral?" She quickly summarized her plan.

"Lawd! Let's get them others, then give me a couple hours. It just might work."

Professional mourners, women hired for their ability to wail and feel the spirit, gathered outside the church. One woman held a large cross fashioned from oak flooring boards and begged for forgiveness on their souls. She shouted her prayers so God would be certain to hear. Well-worn beads and brightly polished bells strung with colored ribbons adorned her cross. When the spirit moved her, she shook the cross until every bead rattled and all the bells chimed. The spirit tended to move strongest when the pay was best and the caretaker had been generous.

"Ain't gettin' in no casket afore I'm dead." Hercules started to sweat. "Ain't right tempting fate." He backed away from the coffin.

"No other way of getting through town," Rachel said. "Kentucky's still a slave state. The way that bounty hunter spreading money around, won't take long till someone tells him something we don't want him to know."

"Huh?"

"He's already got people watching the roads and rivers. What are we gonna do now he's got dawgs?"

"I hates dawgs more'n I hates being wet." Hercules tilted his head to the side and stared at the nearest casket. "But why's it always got to be little spaces? And dark?"

"I don't know, Hercules. I'm praying everybody is gonna think it's them inside." She nodded in the direction of the other rooms where three people awaited burial, "and hoping nobody finds out it's us."

He eased a couple of steps backward and looked ready to run. "We getting inside with dead people?"

"No. Trading places."

"What if the Devil don't realize I ain't dead?"

"He won't be doing the carrying."

"Been praying like a convert, and I gets a box. Gets a death box."

"You blaming me or God?"

"It matter?" His face was shiny and sweat circles formed beneath his armpits.

"Breathe, Hercules." Aveta placed one hand on his chest and the other on his back. "C'mon, now. Take a deep breath."

"Like teasing the Devil, locking me in a death box. What if God don't realize I ain't dead?"

"No lock." Rachel pointed to the side of the casket. "Do your praying to God and remind Him you're still alive."

"Devil don't know that."

"And I ain't telling him. Right now, I'm worried about Samuel. He's just a baby. He don't know better about being quiet."

"Hercules, you can do this." Aveta lowered her voice. "We come this far. Just got to get a little farther—besides, bounty hunter catches you, you'll wish you was dead."

Rachel silently started to count to ten before speaking. It was that or lose what little was left of her patience. *One, two, three ... six, seven–*"Get in that coffin! I'm telling, not asking."

"Hercules," Aveta gently pushed against his chest and tried to move him toward the coffin. "It just a box. Don't mean nothing."

"Get in." Rachel picked up a candlestick and gripped the thin end so she could use it as a club.

"Now hold on, Miss Rachel." He raised his arms in defense.

"Now!"

Some of the fight left him, replaced by shock. "You ain't really gonna hit me, is you?"

"Maybe. But I ain't going back and you ain't taking me with you."

"Get in the box." Aveta gently guided him toward the coffin. "Gonna be all right. I promise."

Hercules shied away. "Don't be making no promises you can't keep."

"When we get on the other side of town, you coming out first," Rachel assured him. "But remember, nobody but the mortician knows we inside. Nobody! You don't make a sound till he lets you out..."

Pall bearers carried Rachel and Samuel, Hercules and Aveta through the streets and white neighborhoods of Lawrenceburg, Kentucky. Rachel and Samuel hid in the first casket, the one closest to the musicians in case he started to cry. It took six men to carry Hercules' coffin, and they traded off with the musicians when their arms got tired. The trumpet player had a bad leg and walked with a limp. He wasn't in the casket-carrying rotation but made up for it by playing the loudest. What he lacked in skill, he made up for in volume. Loud half notes and shrill riffs bounced haphazardly between octaves.

Listening from within her coffin, Rachel imagined his cheeks swelled up the way a lovesick bullfrog will during mating season. *He couldn't hit a pure note with a sledgehammer, but he sure is loud.*

Rachel had peeked through the curtain before getting in the coffin. The Voodoo Princess was a tall, thin woman wearing a purple turban atop her head. An ivory fetish that resembled a braided rope pierced her nose. Animal skins stretched across the top and bottom of a hollow gourd the Princess said was filled with turkey bones. Now, Rachel listened as the woman sang, "Spirits dancing in de graveyard," while shaking the gourd; the sound of skeletons dancing poured forth. "I hear dem bones moving," she shouted. "Dey coming for to carry us home!"

A brass quartet abused instruments chosen for sound production rather than tonal quality. The caskets traveled down the middle of Main Street, passed directly in front of escaped-slave notices bearing descriptions of the people hidden inside, but if Bo Magruder was nearby, he held his hands over his ears.

The procession drew to a rambunctious halt at the cemetery on the edge of town, where a man with the trained voice of a preacher promised everlasting life to those not yet dead. The professional mourners earned their pay with enough grief to store for future use and unnerved those not yet dead. The musicians played somber music as the caskets were lowered into the ground, but now the tears were real, and they came from the people inside the caskets. Dirt pounded against the lid of Rachel's casket and all the irony and humor disappeared.

Trapped! Lawd, what was I thinking? Rachel dug at the lid with her fingers until her nails broke. Samuel sensed her terror and screamed. Her immediate reaction was to beat against the coffin lid or cover her ears, but her panic yielded to maternal instinct and she tried to comfort her baby. She covered his mouth with one hand and clutched him to her chest with the other.

"Shhh. Gonna be alright," she cooed, but didn't believe it. "We getting out of here real soon. Don't you worry, baby. *Got worry enough for both of us…and some left over, besides.*

"Praise Jesus! Thank you Lawd. Getting down on my knees to show you I means it."

She recognized Hercules' voice, muffled, but there was no mistaking his gratitude. She heard scratching from above her casket. "You hang on, Miss Rachel." Hercules rapped on the lid. "All the white folk is gone. We gonna git you out next."

A rush of light and air flooded the casket when Hercules opened the lid. She'd never breathed air so pure or seen a sky so blue. Blood pooled along the edges of her fingernails—the ones she had left. She'd torn two fingernails completely off and blood was smeared across Samuel's face and on his lips. She turned away to hide her shame.

"Don't feel bad, Miss Rachel. Locked inside a casket almost have me wishing for a boat." Hercules wiped nervous sweat from his face. "Held my hands together to keep from trying to get out."

"Everybody scared, just show it in different ways." Rachel washed her hands a few feet away in the nearby stream. "Samuel cried some, but nobody heard him when that trumpet started up."

"That trumpet player so loud, still hear ringing in my ears," Aveta said. "Thank you Miss Rachel."

"You welcome," Rachel breathed a sigh of relief. "Rest up. I'll take the first watch."

"Being scared must take a lot of work. Feel so tired, can't hardly keep my eyes open." Aveta leaned over to where Hercules sat and crossed her arms to form a pillow on his lap.

He didn't look entirely comfortable but made no effort to withdraw, either. He saw Rachel watching and looked sheepish, but managed a bashful smile before he looked away.

And best of luck to you. No reason two people shouldn't have another chance together. Samuel reached for her neck and put his arms around her. He quieted in her arms. *Something about my heartbeat, maybe.* He unerringly came to rest where she could feel his little heart beating about twice as fast as hers.

Lord, help Joe escape so our baby can have his father back. Keep all of us strong so Samuel can grow up his own man instead of another man's property.

She faced south so her coat transferred the sun's heat and sat beneath a stand of loblolly pines with a cushion of long, fragrant needles. Rows of tombstones and simple crosses shielded her from view. The bounty hunter was tricky, like all bounty hunters, but the colored cemetery was one of the last places on earth he would willingly visit. She waited.

Never get used to the waiting. Don't guess this trip's gonna be any different. More hiding than running, more waiting than leaving. Being scared is about the only thing there's plenty enough of.

Brittle clumps of leaves clung to a pin oak, holding on until the last days of spring. A few brave songbirds returned to the tops of trees and traded melodies. The smell of slowly decaying fallen leaves and the feel of the wind as it brushed against her cheek held a faint promise of spring and the rebirth of hope. Honest men might be seldom, but they were one stop, one station, one day closer to Canada and true freedom. It was enough for now.

CHAPTER NINE

A fair breeze carried the slow clip-clop of mules as they pulled a heavy wagon. Hercules softly snored and Aveta was asleep. Samuel rested in Rachel's arms. *Don't sound like a bounty hunter.*

She peeked through the leafy branches that concealed them. The man riding atop the wagon had dark, bushy hair going gray on top. He wore faded overalls and a battered straw hat. She held still and let her top eye watch him draw near. Her life and three others' depended on what it saw.

The wagon stopped just the other side of the cemetery and she gasped. "What are you doing here?"

"Helping." He looked her way, but couldn't see her through the thick foliage.

"How can I trust you?"

"Already trusted me once." He stepped down from the wagon. "My conscience wouldn't let me alone, so I come back."

"Then it's about time I know your name." Rachel looked both ways and stepped away from her cover.

"Deacon Turner," the farmer said. He extended a callused hand in greeting.

"Rachel." She grasped his hand with both of hers. "I promise I'll repay this favor if God gives me another chance."

"God willing," he said. "Meanwhile, let's get you across the Ohio River. Freedom's waiting."

She walked down to the stream where they'd been hiding. "Aveta. Hercules, wake up." She motioned for them to follow her toward the wagon.

"Got me a load of bricks, this time." Deacon Turner pointed toward his wagon.

"I know you," Hercules said. "You the man with the barn."

"That's right. You can call me Deacon Turner."

"Thought you wasn't willing to do no more." Hercules motioned for Rachel to step away from the wagon. He turned sideways and whispered, "How we know he ain't changed his mind about collecting the reward?"

"How we know he ain't the answer to our prayers?"

"Huh?"

"We got to keep moving, Hercules," she whispered back, although Deacon Turner stood within hearing range. "We all out of rivers and funerals. Bricks is what we got left."

"Like last time—only better." Deacon Turner said. "I'll leave an opening in the middle. Stack these bricks around you. Nobody gonna know you in the middle."

"You ain't answered my question," Hercules said. "Why you changing your mind?"

"Nothing left for me to go back to." Deacon Turner looked away and wiped tears from both eyes. "When I come back from dropping you off, my house was burnt up. Buried my wife and children—wasn't nothing left but three lumps of ashes and bone—two of them almost too tiny to find." His shoulders sagged. He bent over from the pain, braced his hands against his knees and took deep breaths. "Must be some reason God don't want me dead. I got to go on."

"You sure?" Aveta moved away from the wagon to comfort him. "About going on, I mean."

"Got the rest of my life to grieve."

Aveta rested a hand on his shoulder. "Never knew my daddy. Lost my mama when I was too young to remember, but I seen enough family sold to know about pain. Reckon a year or two of forgetting the little things is about all that helps with the hurt."

"Maybe. Pain ain't no stranger."

"Sorry about your family—lost most of my own, and I don't mean to be ungrateful...but them bricks looks like them little houses where white folk is buried." Hercules frowned and shook his head as he did whenever there were tight spaces involved.

"How long we staying inside this time?" Aveta asked.

"Long as it takes," Rachel said.

"Another death box." Hercules wrapped his arms around his head and moaned. "Enough to make a man stop praying."

"It's the price of freedom, Hercules. Always a little more than you figure on paying," Deacon Turner said.

Aveta turned worried eyes to Rachel. "You think this'll work the way them caskets did, Miss Rachel? Think nobody's gonna be looking for us in there?"

"They're looking for you everywhere." Deacon Turner's frown said he'd had enough talk. "No other way to get you north."

"Guess I'd better help." Hercules reached for a brick.

"Just the top two layers," Deacon Turner said. "The center is hollow. I'll restack the top rows when you're inside."

"Looks awful small." Aveta said.

"Looks awful dark." Hercules groaned, and looked longingly at the sun. "How we gonna breathe?"

"Air's gonna come through here." Deacon Turner pointed out the offset bricks in the inner shell. They formed a diamond pattern of evenly spaced openings.

"Not much air," Aveta said. "Not enough for three people and a baby."

"Don't know that for certain," Rachel said. "Only way to find out is get inside. Nobody gonna think of looking for us in there. All that matters."

"Maybe." Aveta leaned over the side of the wagon and peered inside the cell. "Maybe not, but it ain't like we got much choice."

"What do you call them graves on top of the ground?" Hercules asked.

"A mausoleum?" Deacon Turner offered.

"That's it. Praying like a convert for no more death boxes, and gets put in a mausoleum with two women and a baby."

Deacon Turner couldn't quite hide his smile. "The Lord works in mysterious ways, Hercules."

"Or He taking a nap and not working at all."

The inner cell was too short for Hercules to lie flat. It was too narrow for all three of them to sit side by side, and too low for sitting hunched over and opposite one another. The only way they could all fit inside was to lie on their sides, bend at the waist and curl their legs into a fetal position. Rachel curled around Samuel, Aveta came next, and Hercules squeezed inside around all three. "Feel like a big spoon in a narrow drawer," he said. "Ain't praying no more. God likely to hear me and come up with something worse."

Deacon Turner stacked the loose bricks across the back of the wagon. Each tier blocked out a little more light and a little more of the available fresh air. After the first row was in place, Rachel couldn't hear the songbirds. The second row silenced everything but Aveta's irregular breathing and Hercules' moans.

"Quit moaning, Hercules. Breathe through your nose, Aveta. Rachel! You got to keep that baby quiet. And all of you, shush up."

The wagon rocked slightly as Deacon Turner climbed up to the seat and grabbed hold of the reins. "Hah. Pull!" The wheels creaked and groaned as they rolled over uneven ground, but the ride was smoother once they reached the roadway and the mules settled into a comfortable pace. They plodded along the turnpike. It might have been an hour. It seemed longer to Rachel. It was hard to tell locked away from the sun, but to Hercules, it must have seemed an eternity. Samuel soiled his diaper. If there was any air left inside, it wasn't fit for humans.

"Can't breathe! Let me out," Hercules screamed.

"Quiet." Rachel's arms were wedged at her sides; she couldn't reach his mouth to muffle his shouts. "You got to stay quiet!"

"Help! Help!" In full panic, Hercules tried to kick the bricks loose. When he couldn't dislodge the bricks set with mortar, he clawed at the bricks on the opposite side, the ones merely stacked in place. Their hiding place crumbled.

"Hah! Get up there," Deacon Turner called. The wagon bounced and pitched when they left the roadway.

The wagon tilted forward and picked up speed as it rolled downhill. The mules lost their footing. The lullaby of their rhythmic hoof beats changed tempo and woke Samuel. He whimpered when their hooves clattered against the rocks in a desperate attempt to regain control.

More bricks fell to the ground as Hercules struggled free. The wagon leaned precariously close to tipping over when it crossed the uneven terrain. Rachel and Aveta were thrown to the downward side, and all of Hercules' weight compacted them from above, then transferred to Samuel who began to wail.

"C'mon. Pull!" Deacon Turner yelled. The wagon righted itself, then just as quickly tipped in the opposite direction. When they were thrown to the other side, this time it was Hercules crushed beneath everyone's weight.

"Whoa!" Deacon Turner shouted. The wagon veered off the road and Rachel hit her head against the bricks stacked above her. Sunlight filtered through the gap left behind by the impact when she landed on her back. Samuel started to cry.

The mules brayed in desperation. The wagon stopped bouncing. Rachel heard Aveta and Hercules take a deep breath. Samuel tensed against her chest.

Huh? Feels like my body is froze stiff, but I don't 'member getting cold. There ain't no noise. No bouncing. Nuthin.

The bricks above her head scattered when the wagon's brief flight ended with a disastrous landing. The impact thrust her upper body forward, but she managed to turn her shoulder toward the front of the wagon so she wouldn't crush Samuel. She slammed into the bricks stacked in the front of the wagon. Her head snapped forward hard enough to make her neck hurt, her nose inches away from the wagon's bench seat. She saw a patch of blue sky and the bottom of Deacon Turner's boot where a hole had been worn beneath the big toe.

"Whoa!" Deacon Turner lost hold of the reins and slid off the seat, but the leather straps were looped around his wrist. The mules dragged him on the ground but the effect was to turn the wagon in a half-circle so they faced uphill. The wagon slowed, and then shuddered to a stop partway up the steep incline.

"Let me outta this death box," Hercules burrowed his way from beneath the bricks. He reached over Rachel's back and grabbed the back of the seat to pull himself free, but didn't notice Samuel who was pinned beneath him.

"Hercules," Rachel screamed. "Stop." She arched her back and yanked his hands off the seat.

"Let go of me Satan!" Hercules reached over her shoulders and grabbed the bottom of the seat.

Samuel wailed. Rachel dropped to her knees. She bent forward and pulled Samuel into the protective hollow formed between her shoulders and knees. When she tried to push Hercules off her back, her hands slipped off his chin and struck his neck. Blood roared against her eardrums—it sounded like dogs howling. She tightened her grip. The outside world disappeared. All she could see was red. Hercules clawed at Rachel's hands but she was lost in her nightmares and couldn't let go.

A trail of bricks knocked loose from the wagon led toward the road. A low-hanging branch from a dogwood tree was wedged between the wagon and its irregularly shaped load of bricks. The inner cell was intact, but every corner and most of the sides were in disarray. Zigzag patterns of missing bricks dominated the once tidy load. The mules whinnied as the wagon inched downhill. Deacon Turner scrambled to his knees, but he had landed too far down the hill to grab the reins. Aveta was trapped beneath the haphazard load of bricks remaining in the wagon. The mules reared as the wagon pulled them backward. Hercules lunged for their halters when their front legs touched the ground.

"Whoa," Hercules said. "Settle down, now." Gently, he pulled on the halter and eased the mules backward, let the weight of the wagon pull them to a stop on semi-level ground.

Deacon Turner brushed the dirt from the front of his clothes. "You're good with animals," he gasped.

"Yes, sir," Hercules rubbed his bruised throat. "Get me off a boat or out of a death box, I do just fine. With my feet on the ground or reins in my hand, I ain't no trouble at all." He handed Deacon Turner the reins and helped Aveta climb out of the wagon.

Aveta rubbed the dirt out of her eyes. "Miss Rachel?"

Aveta's voice sounded fuzzy.

"You okay?" Hercules asked. "Miss Rachel?"

Why's Hercules shimmering like he's underwater? We drowning?

"Look like she in some kind of trance." Deacon Turner said.

Rachel cupped her hand behind her ear. *He's saying something, but his words is running together like he ain't got no air. He drowning, too?*

"Seen my wife get like this when our youngest died. She just couldn't—"

Are we in heaven? "Samuel?"

"He's okay, Miss Rachel." Aveta touched her cheek. "You holding him."

Rachel stared at her hands. Samuel looked back at her. "Up? Dada?"

"Grandma? Joe?" Rachel squinted her eyes against the sun. "Why everybody underwater?"

"Looks like she's seeing something horrible," Aveta said, "like she can't look away."

"I think she's in a trance," Deacon Turner said.

"It's them bricks. I know just how she feels. C'mon Miss Rachel." With the same gentle tone he used on the mules, Hercules led her toward the wagon. "Sit here while we pick up these bricks."

"Dawgs," Rachel muttered. "I hear them howling. Smell the fur burning."

"She having visions?" Aveta asked.

"Or she's stuck in some kind'a bad dream." Hercules wrapped his arms around her and pinned her hands to her sides. "She gonna hurt herself for sure, she keep going on."

"Joe? Is that you, Joe?"

"It's me, Miss Rachel. Hercules. Wake up."

"Don't think she understand you." Aveta waved her hand in front of Rachel's face. When that didn't work, she snapped her fingers.

"What? Joe?"

Deacon Turner said. "Let her go, Hercules."

"What if she drop Samuel? Ain't sure she even know he's in her arms." He helped her walk to a nearby stump where she could sit. Walking brought her back to them.

"What happened?"

"You was out of your mind," Hercules said.

"Or maybe trapped in a bad dream," Aveta added. "We wasn't sure what to do."

"You was saying something 'bout dawgs," Hercules said, looking around. "You hearing dawgs, Miss Rachel?"

"Seeing them with my top eye. Where are we?"

"Not rightly sure," Deacon Turner admitted. "Ain't never been this far north."

"Feels like we ain't far enough." Rachel said. "That bounty hunter bound to catch up with us. Not that many roads. We tried everything else. Overheard the Missus talking about a station at Frankfort. Reckon the train about the only chance we got left now that he's got dawgs."

"How we gonna get on a train?" Aveta asked.

"Tight spaces and a leaky boat. Death boxes and maus'leums." Hercules put his arms over his head and moaned. "After all that, I gets caught by dawgs."

Rachel was still for several heartbeats before she looked around her. She glanced down at hands. Her eyes settled on Samuel and her top eye came into focus. "We ain't caught yet, Hercules. And I ain't goin' back; ain't having my baby raised a slave." She looked at the ruined pile of bricks, then at the trees nearby. "If we leave these bricks here and find some wood..."

If anyone cared to notice, the old woman was one of those overlooked, forgotten slaves who existed just outside the periphery of society. She hunched her back and kept her head tilted down, kept her eyes downcast so nobody would notice her eyes shifting from side to side or detect the long lashes belonging to a young woman. Rachel held the reins with both hands and kept her sleeves pulled over her fingers lest someone notice her skin was untouched by age spots or distended veins.

The massive crate on the back of the wagon was crudely fashioned from weathered lumber, discreet air holes carved into the corners where the boards met. The crate was cramped inside, but Aveta insisted she was used to it. Hercules was sedated with the only drug readily available: skullcap. It looked like a weed, but Rachel promised there would be no ill effects—she wouldn't give it to Samuel; he was too young, but she didn't tell Hercules about her concerns. Clean and fed, Samuel went right to sleep after she bound him to her back with a scarf. The loose-fitting coat she borrowed from Deacon Turner hid Samuel from view and turned her feminine physique into an indistinct lump.

They'd stopped on the edge of Frankfort and sent Deacon Turner on ahead to purchase a train ticket and arrange shipping, acting under the guise of a slave making arrangements for his master. Rachel followed with the wagon. She avoided the station and stopped the wagon at the freight dock, where workers unloaded the crate and placed it on a baggage car.

It was a long train, and the dock sat at the far end of the station. She was stopped for less than a minute but she was upwind. Above the bustling noises, she heard braying dogs.

"Stop her," came a familiar shout. "Escaped slave!"

Rachel recognized the red hair and bulky shoulders. A chill that had little to do with the day's frigid cold enveloped her. The bounty hunter was at the station. The dogs strained against their leashes until the leather straps choked off their howls.

"Hah! Get on," she yelled, urging the mules to pull hard left. As she did, she risked another glance at the ticket window and saw the bounty hunter release the dogs.

The train's whistle sounded. She heard the conductor call out, "All aboard! Move along, people. Nothing more to see here."

When she was clear of the station, she glanced over her shoulder. Deacon Turner stood on the platform as the train pulled away from the station. *He wouldn't be standing there if they was unloading the box. Means Hercules and Aveta on their way to Canady. Good. Samuel and me is still free and we ain't going back.*

"Hah! C'mon on now. Pull!" She flicked the reins and wished for fast horses, but these were mules, bred for strength not speed.

Slavery was still legal in Kentucky, but the Union Army controlled the trains; no one helped her, but no one interfered with her flight. It wasn't enough. The bounty hunter owned stallions. The dogs howled. It wouldn't take them long to catch her. *Unless...*

"Whoa." She pulled back on the reins and brought the wagon to a stop in the middle of a bridge. She removed the stuffing from beneath her clothes and threw it in the back of the wagon, unwrapped her scarf and added it to the pile. With any luck, the dogs would track the scent on her discarded clothes.

"Get on home," she yelled and turned the reins loose. "Go on, now. Hah!" The mules pulled, and she jumped from the wagon bed into the cold waters of the Kentucky River.

CHAPTER TEN

Rachel plunged into the icy Kentucky River with an explosion of light green bubbles. The loose clothing she wore helped slow her descent, but she went deeper into the water than sunlight penetrated. She shed her coat and felt the heavy, waterlogged material snag against Samuel's head, felt him fight his way free by kicking his legs against her back. She clawed her way toward the surface. A kaleidoscope of refracted light confused her; the disorienting prism of rainbows made her reach for the surface long before she bumped up against the ice. She pushed against the underside of the frozen mass, but this sent her deeper underwater. She beat against the ice with her fists until her knuckles bled. When that didn't work, she tried to punch a hole through with her elbow. The effort only pushed her farther beneath the surface.

She bent forward and reached over her shoulders to unwrap Samuel. The top of her head crashed against the ice sheet. A comforting lethargy enveloped her and pushed aside the cold. Red spots filled her view to the surface. *Is this what passing over to the other side is like?* The river lulled her with its relentless dull roar. *Is this what Grandma saw?* A few drops of water seeped past her lips and trickled toward her lungs. *Is this what she felt? Keep your fire and brimstone, Satan. Hell's full of ice-cold water and bloodhounds.*

Something tickled her feet. *Strange. Is this what drowning is like?* She thought of Grandma, how she used to tickle her feet when she got so sad, nothing else could make her laugh. *Used to laugh so hard, couldn't hardly breathe. Can't help it. Got to kick my feet before she tickles me to death.*

She kicked her feet and struck the river bottom. Instinct made her bend her legs, push off against the bottom of the river and extend her arms toward the surface so Samuel could breathe. He kicked his legs against her arms—she nearly dropped him. The current carried them downstream to a bend in the river where the channel was deeper and the water flowed too fast for ice to form. Her hands broke the surface. Samuel coughed the water out of his lungs while she rolled onto her back so she could keep her arms out of the water. Samuel was coughing too hard to cry. She arched her back, tilted her head backward so her face was out of the water, and gasped for air with the desperation of a woman who has one foot in hell.

Her waterlogged clothing dragged her beneath the surface again, so she kicked off her shoes and let the swift current help angle her toward shore. With a few feeble strokes, she used the river to help carry her toward a bend where there was shallow water. Too weak to stand, she crawled ashore where scraggly chokecherry bushes and bayberry shrubs grew near the water's edge. Thorns tore at her exposed skin, but she was too cold to feel their sting. She crawled halfway out of the water and collapsed on the muddy slope. When the river tugged her legs downstream and tried to float her back in, she wrapped the fingers of her right hand around the branches and held tight until enough strength returned to pull her body fully ashore.

The foliage hid her from view, but the shivers hit so hard she shook the leaves. Samuel cried from the cold. The dogs yipped with the thrill of reacquiring their scent—or recognizing Samuel's cries. With a howl they drew closer.

"Shush-up now, Samuel," she tried to comfort him. "Be a good boy and quiet down."

He held out his arms for Joe. He took a deep breath, turned down his lip and wailed.

She rocked him in her arms, tickled his feet, but he needed a nap or for Joe to throw him in the air. She pressed her hand against his mouth and pulled him toward her chest until she could feel the soft bones on the back of his skull move inward. He wailed from the pain and didn't stop struggling. He kicked his heels against her stomach, beat his fists against her chest.

A bloodhound brayed. "Over there," a man shouted.

"Got 'em." Another man, with a deeper voice answered.

She took a deep breath and plunged into the river. She held Samuel above the water and swam with one arm. He wouldn't stop crying. The dogs heard him and ran to the river's edge. She swam as hard as she could, paddled her legs furiously, but the current pulled them toward the shore. The dogs raced ahead to a bend in the river and splashed into the water.

The lead dog bared his fangs and started swimming toward them. The other dogs followed.

Rachel yanked Samuel to her chest and ducked underneath the surface just before the lead dog reached them. She heard his teeth smash together when he narrowly missed Samuel's forearm and bit down on nothing but water. She swam beneath the surface of the river where the dogs couldn't follow her.

Hang on Samuel. She sent him her thoughts so he would understand. *We got to get away from these dawgs or we both gonna die. Swimming underwater the only way. Won't be long. I promise.*

She heard men shouting, cursing, felt one dog bite her ankle, but she kicked him in the snout and he let go. Samuel wouldn't stop screaming. Two of the dogs splashed ashore and ran ahead to the next bend in the river.

She clutched Samuel to her chest, lowered her head and swam beneath the river's surface. Samuel beat his fists against her chest and kicked her in the stomach with his feet as he struggled to breathe. He screamed, but the sound didn't penetrate the surface and the dogs couldn't hear him. The blows from his tiny fists slowed, his kicks became steadily weaker. She felt him coughing the water out of his lungs, saw the water beneath her chin froth with his spasms, felt the warmth of his blood, saw the water turn pink, but the dogs couldn't hear him.

She swept her arm through the water, held Samuel with one arm and paddled with the other. When her arms were too tired to swim, she kicked with her feet and let the current carry them downstream. When her legs began to cramp, she fought her way to shore and crawled out of the river. Samuel didn't cry. He was a good boy and lay perfectly still—didn't move, didn't make a sound.

⚞ ⚟

Rachel moaned in her sleep, shifted her legs to get comfortable and woke herself up. She squinted her eyes against the bright sunshine. She looked around, then down. The back of her throat and the bottom of her lungs hurt. She swallowed a mouthful of soot. Her first conscious breath carried more smoke than air. The scorched ground she sat on was a cornfield once, but now there were burnt stalks and furrows filled with ash. Her dress was stained from the alkaline soil. A small band of gold circled her waist where the drawstring cinched, but the muddy river water had saturated the rest of the fabric, leaving behind a deposit of sedimentary clay and silt. A mere hint of gold remained visible in a narrow crease beneath her collar. Blood seeped from her ankle and formed stark red rivulets that pushed aside the silt and gray ash caked on her battered feet.

"Is this hell?"

"It was three days ago." A stocky man with a pock-marked black face and gray hair removed his straw hat and held it to his chest. "Now the Union Troops calling it a victory."

"Where's Samuel?"

"Don't you remember?" He bent over and peered at her face.

"I—the dawgs. I remember the dawgs. Most everything else a—a waking kind of nightmare. Where's my baby?"

Three long heartbeats passed before he spoke again. "Maybe it's better that way. You probably better off not knowing.

"Who are you?" He wore faded overalls. His red-checked shirt was patched with tan broadcloth. His shirt collar was worn through in two places and the sleeves were frayed at the cuffs.

"You don't remember? You sure?"

Rachel shook her head. "Last I remember, Grandma was tickling my feet."

"We already met—Deacon Turner, ma'am." Smallpox scars, some of them too deep for his beard to disguise, marked both cheeks. His forehead showed similar scarring. "That's my wagon you leaning up against—you was driving it three days ago. The rest... Well, maybe you better off forgetting."

"What happened? Where am I?"

"You near the Kentucky River. About 10 miles downstream of Frankfort. Union Army and Confederates been fighting each other off and on for three days, now. Confederates is calling it a victory but they done retreated. Union Army still around, but I ain't taking no chances—hiding from both sides for three days now."

"Three days?" She leaned forward and rubbed her ankles. "The lightning went away, but I think—mighta heard thunder for three days."

"Cannons. You was hearing the fighting." Frowning made his bushy eyebrows form a continuous, furry stripe across the ridgeline above his eyes. Pronounced ridges on the top of his skull gave his head a segmented look. "They ain't shooting at each other no more."

Where bomb craters pockmarked the field, corpses lay in semicircles as if carefully arranged by an unseen hand. Clouds of flies circled above lifeless bodies. Windblown ash obscured the view beyond the battlefield, except for the shadowy outline of a lone tree that somehow escaped being chopped down for use in the ramparts lining the edge of the battlefield. A row of recently felled trees had been set into the ground at an angle and pointed south toward enemy lines. The faint smell of freshly chopped wood lingered in the piles of bark beneath the crudely sharpened ends, but the overwhelming stench of decay hung above the rotting corpses strewn haphazardly along the battlefield. Tattered blue and gray strips of clothing fluttered from between a few of the points as a whirlwind swirled a column of gray and black ash skyward.

She turned her head away and waited for the spiraling debris to pass. Ash swirled around her, covered her lips with dust. She opened her eyes to blink away the grit after the dust devil passed.

"Samuel, your baby—I'm sorry. Want me to take him, take the body out of your hands?"

"No! He just needs to get warm. See? His lips ain't hardly blue no more. The little purple and red dots is almost gone."

"Hmm." He leaned forward and waved his hand in front of her face. "You still shook up from the battle. I seen it before. You safe, for now. You free. Ain't seen hide nor hair of that bounty hunter once the fighting start up."

She cradled Samuel's head in the crook of her elbow and extended her hands. "Free? Look at these hands! I ain't never getting free."

"I see your poor hands is rubbed raw. Looks like your fingers is maybe hurt some, too, but they ain't bleeding." He rummaged among the bodies piled in the wagon. "Here. Put on these gloves."

"They're bloody!"

"Nah. Just dirty. If it was blood, fingers would be stuck together."

"No. My hands. There's blood on my hands. See?"

He peered at her hands, then her eyes. "I see you been having a rough time of it. You safe now." He held out the gloves. "You made it. You free."

She cradled Samuel's cold body against her chest. "I'll get you warm, child," she cooed. "Then everything gonna be okay."

"Rachel?" He leaned forward. "Can you hear me?"

"Just need a blanket. Maybe some water."

His smile faded into a sorrowful frown of compassion. "Where's my manners? You been swimming in the Kentucky River, not drinking it."

"No. To wash my hands. See?" She held out the palms of her bloody hands so he could see.

"Awful sorry for your loss. Know just how you feel. Want me to take him for you?"

"I got to wash my hands. I just, I just got to wash off the blood."

"I know you hurting for your child. Buried my wife and two children. Lost everybody. Broke my heart, but God don't want me dead, yet. Got to keep on."

"He just need to warm up."

"I can help you to warm up. But there ain't nothing I can do for your baby. And you being little more'n a child yourself. Crying shame."

"Can't get the blood off my hands."

"You must be stuck in some kinda bad dream. My wife got the same way when we lost our first-born. Get you some rest—"

She pressed Samuel to her chest with one hand and placed her other palm on the burnt earth. She tried to curl her legs underneath her so she could stand, but managed only one knee before nausea overtook her. The ground rippled beneath her. Everything turned blurry like she'd been spinning herself dizzy.

Something wrong with my feet. Can't feel my toes. Got to keep running.

She saw a tall black man reaching for her. She couldn't see his face, but he held a corncob pipe in his left hand and it smelled of tobacco, the same leaf Grandma used to smoke.

"That you, Grandma," she mumbled. "I know you here beside me. Ain't give up. Much as I wanted too— ain't give up cause you wouldn't like it." Her knee buckled. "Help me keep running, Grandma," she shouted. The dogs howled, their cries echoed in her ears. Her right leg was stronger and she could limp to the river. The dogs couldn't follow her there.

Her left knee struck the ground, but she couldn't push herself upright for fear of dropping Samuel. She half spun and struck her head against the wagon. Things slowed down and got fuzzy, like the time the Missus broke a vase against her head and she'd been sleepy for three days. A translucent fog enveloped the sun. It grew quiet in a soft, comforting sort of way, like when Grandma would hug her and hold her until she stopped crying. An ethereal stillness settled all around her. For a moment, she was at peace. She collapsed, and the injured side of her head struck the ground.

Grandma took Rachel's hand. A comforting void beckoned, free of physical restraints and the burden of self. There was water here, flowing with a supple calm. Evergreens and herbs grew nearby—unfamiliar but fragrant, alluring. Grandma tugged on her arm, tickled her feet when she didn't want to leave. Samuel held out his arms and Grandma threw him in the air. He laughed and Rachel knew Joe must be nearby.

Her clothes felt heavy. She lowered her head and noticed she was wearing men's trousers and a coarse woolen shirt. The collar scratched her neck. She reached up to pull it away. A black man, nearly as big as Joe, but older, was staring at her. She scrambled backward but a wagon wheel blocked her escape. She raised one arm in defense and felt behind her for a weapon. *Nothing but ashes.*

"Can you hear me? Hello? You passed out. Crumpled to the ground like a half-empty sack 'a taters."

"Samuel. My baby. He gotta be hungry. Where is he?"

"You don't remember a thing, do you? You was out of your mind. Seeing things. Talking to somebody named Grandma—yelling about seein' blood on your hands. Wouldn't let go of that baby till you passed out. Just lean back against this wagon."

Dead bodies were stacked in the wagon: four-by-four-by-eight, about the size of a cord of wood. The stench would have made her vomit but there didn't seem to be anything in her stomach. Just a little bit of bile came up. "Oh God! Where's Samuel?"

"You free. Understand? Confederates on the run. We ain't far from the Union Army camps and that bounty hunter be avoiding both of them."

"Samuel! Where is he?" she asked, but she knew.

She looked at her hands and saw fingers that had held her son underwater until he drowned. Was that dirt or dried blood beneath her nails? Samuel had coughed up too much blood for the water to wash all of the stain away. A tremor passed through her hands. She curled her fingers and clenched her hands into fists until her nails bit into her palms.

Bruises covered her forearms, left behind by Samuel's small heels where he had kicked her in his struggle to survive. Tears formed in her eyes until her vision turned blurry, the way it had looked underwater while she was hiding from the dogs. She blinked and the tear drops that rolled down her cheeks carried the memory of Samuel's traumatic death. She brushed away the tears, felt the warmth against the back of her hand and remembered how the blood Samuel had coughed up from his lungs was just as warm. Her hands shook with the memory so she put them behind her back and out of sight, but the image of his blood remained.

She had killed her own son to survive.

"Guess the price of getting north is leaving somebody behind. We all lost somebody."

"I lost—everybody." The words tumbled out. "Mama, sold downriver. Grandma, worked to death. Joe might as well be dead—less he finds his courage. Samuel. Oh God, my baby." She covered her face. No soap, no amount of hand-washing would remove the memory of Samuel's death from her murderous fingers. "No!"

"Sorry for your child. Seem like the cost of freedom always more'n we can afford to pay."

She wailed, "I don't want my baby stacked on that wagon like a piece of wood."

"No ma'am. Course not."

"That your shovel in the back of the wagon?"

"Is now. Confederate Army left it behind when they retreated."

A massive pin oak grew along the bank of the Kentucky River, near the mouth of a creek too small to have a name. Rachel stood on the shovel to push the dull blade through the packed soil. There were kernels of corn in the first few shovelfuls of dirt, but the topsoil was shallow. A few more shovelfuls revealed reddish clay and roots as thick as her arm.

"Here," he reached for the shovel. "Let me help."

"No. I killed him. I'll bury him." She severed the roots with brutal thrusts of the shovel. Her bloody hands slipped on the worn handle with each jolt. She put the roots aside and kept digging until the hole was deep enough to deter animals intent on unearthing Samuel's body. She split the chopped-up roots into pieces and arranged them in a square to line the edge of the grave. This was to be her baby's home for eternity, earthen wood for a baby buried without a coffin.

She wrapped Samuel in a dead man's coat so the dirt wouldn't lie against his upturned face.

She bowed her head but no prayers would come. She closed her eyes but there were no tears left, either. "I'm sorry," she said. No apology could excuse her crime, but there was nothing else she could offer. "I'm sorry," she repeated. She tilted the shovel so the dirt gently slid off the blade. "I'm so sorry."

Deacon Turner removed his hat but remained silent while she filled the grave, patted the last shovelful onto the tiny mound. He stepped forward to say a few words but she put her arm out to stop him.

"No. Nothing nobody says is gonna make this any better. Nothing left but to keep on." She put her hands behind her back. "Ain't giving up. Grandma wouldn't like it. Which way do I got to run?"

CHAPTER ELEVEN

Rachel waited in the woods on the edge of Frankfort, Kentucky. Deacon Turner stayed in the forest behind her, watching the wagon and keeping the mules silent. With nothing to eat, too far to travel and nowhere left to hide, they couldn't afford to trust anyone, but they were desperate. She crept to the edge of a clearing. If it was a farm, she could find food. If it was a city building, there would be water. She parted the branches of a winterberry bush and peered through the leaves.

A small building sat in the middle of the clearing. One window, a sharply pitched roof, the white cross mounted at the apex of the roof meant this simple structure was a house of worship. *Wonder if they got food or water stored inside?*

She waited. Bounty hunters could be tricky. She waited long enough for any white man hidden nearby to show himself.

I don't hear a thing. A white man or his horse would'a made some noise by now. Don't smell no cigar smoke, no chewing tobacco neither, but best wait a little longer.

After another half hour, her top eye told her it was safe to approach. *There ain't no white men hiding in this forest. A bounty hunter or pattyroller can't stay quiet for this long.*

She crept toward the back of the church, as far away from the front door as possible. She crawled on her hands and knees to stay below the window, and then dropped to her stomach beside the front door. Gently, ever so gently, she twisted the doorknob.

Unlocked! Guess I'm overdue for a miracle.

She eased the door open and pressed her ear against the gap. She listened, heard her own excited breathing but little else.

Nothing. Must mean my luck is changing.

She slipped inside, smelled horses and an unwashed body.

Strange. That ain't right...

She spun on her heels, ducked through the door but not fast enough. The blow missed her head, struck her at the base of the neck and she felt the knuckles in his fist smash against her spine. The next blow knocked her off-balance. She stumbled against a table. The sharp edge struck her in the hip, knocking a lantern onto the floor. The glass shattered. When she pushed off the table to get her balance, one of the legs broke and she crashed to the floor. The door slammed shut and someone kicked her in the hip. The next kick missed her and struck the table.

"Goddamn it to hell!" he yelled, and tried to stomp on her but she scrambled backward, caught a glimpse of red hair in the light coming through the window.

Bounty hunter. Recognize the sickly white skin and the hair lookin' like it's on fire.

He bent his knee and raised his leg to kick her again, but she rolled away. She felt the broken glass beneath her and picked up a shard. She lunged, missed his face, cut a gaping wound in the fleshy underside of his arm.

The sharp fragment was a two-sided blade, though. Blood dripped from her palm. She ignored the wound and swiped at his face but he ducked out of reach.

He circled to his right until he was on the opposite side of the room, then reached for something behind him. He didn't look away. She saw him fumble through a leather sack or maybe his saddlebag. She ran to the door while he was distracted. Locked. She kicked at the lock but the door was solid and it hurt her foot. She aimed her next kick at the hinges, and the wooden frame set into the wall developed a crack. *Couple more kicks, maybe.* She glanced over her shoulder. The bounty hunter held a bottle in one hand.

She kicked the door and felt wood splinter beneath the thin soles of her worn-out shoes. *Just gonna take one more kick.* A foul-smelling liquid drenched her shoulder. Some of it splashed on her neck.

Chloroform. Recognize the smell from the big house doctor.

The door sagged against the broken frame, but the chloroform fumes enveloped her. *Feeling dizzy.* She held her breath. *Still dizzy.*

He picked up a chair and hurled it at her. A chair leg struck her in the head and stunned her into indecisiveness.

Should I kick him or the door? Can't breathe. Got to—

He struck her in the back with his fist and forced the remaining air from her lungs. Another punch landed between her shoulder blades and she couldn't stop herself from inhaling. Chloroform fumes burned into her lungs. She felt the awful embrace of drugged unconsciousness as all the light drained from her body. She fell toward the floor but never felt the impact.

When she regained consciousness, she was in hell. Rope encircled her wrists and elbows and bound her hands behind her back. Her stomach was queasy. The ground rocked beneath her, and she smelled the dank odor of rotting vegetation, felt the swaying undulation of waves and realized she was on the water. She could wiggle her fingers but they felt sluggish and swollen. An iron cuff encircled her left ankle, attached to three feet of rusty chain that led from her ankle to a wooden post stout enough to hold an anchor. Coal dust filled the cracks in the wooden deck. She looked to either side, noticed the low, square walls and realized she was on a barge.

River this big…got to be the Kentucky. Satan sure got a cruel sense of humor, floating me down the river I been following toward freedom.

A bruise in the shape of a boot heel dyed her shin an ugly shade of purple. Her head ached. It hurt to breathe. Her soul mourned the loss of freedom.

"Ain't so uppity now, is ya?" The bounty hunter spit a stream of dark brown tobacco juice near her feet.

She tried to move her feet aside, but the chain was too short. The next stream of tobacco juice splattered against her shins. The cuff had already rubbed her ankle raw, but the hurt went much deeper.

He laughed. "Penny here, nickel or two there, didn't take much money for someone to sell you out. You headed back where you belong."

She was too proud to let him see her despair. A longing for revenge would keep her strong when there was no hope left. She sneered at him. "Little man, how you holding on to so much hate?"

"Nobody talks to Bo Magruder like that. Show some respect or I'll slap that look right off'n your face, whore."

"Ain't no whore any more'n you a man."

"We'll see about that." He reached for his belt buckle. "Time we get to Lexington, have you wishing you was already dead and in hell."

"You ain't the first white man wanting a taste of me. Seen your look plenty of times before. Just like I know there's more'n one black baby running around with a tint of your red hair. Maybe all your little bastard children got them strange green eyes looking like they don't belong. You just like all them other white men—wanting what they ain't supposed to be having."

"Shut up bitch! Time I'm finished with you, you'll be wishin' you was dead."

"Too late. Already wishing that since I woke up in chains."

CHAPTER TWELVE

Three months into a new year and nothing grew around the bell tower where Joe had watched Marse Williams burn the Emancipation Proclamation. Grass grew beneath the split rail fence near the slave quarters and weeds sprouted along once pristine pathways. Tobacco stalks remained in the back fields. The leaves were stripped and hung upside down to dry in the barns, but by the time the few remaining field slaves finished plowing the old plants under, it would be time to plant again.

Joe slid off the bed, heard cornhusks whisper inside the thin ticking. He got down on his knees to pray, figuring God or his angels would hear him better. Words tumbled through his mind, words he couldn't find while he had watched his wife and son slipping out the door. Why didn't he try to stop them? Where was his courage to go with her, to protect Rachel and Samuel while they ran to freedom together? He closed his eyes to fight back the tears; they seeped through anyway. He hadn't cried since he was a little boy. He curled up on the floor and wrapped his arms around his chest. The hurt welled up inside and nothing would stop it from coming out. He sobbed no matter how hard he tried to be a man. He clasped his arms over his head, but the pain didn't go away. *If you listenin', Lord, please send Rachel some help.*

The first exploratory drops of windblown rain played a staccato stanza upon the tin roof. The storm gathered force; a percussive symphony pounded through the walls and ceiling. Hail turned the thin metal roof into a makeshift church bell and pealed out a call for prayer. *Sounds like God is listening. Please deliver Rachel and Samuel to the North—an if it ain't too late, give me some courage to follow her.*

The storm eventually passed, but he kept praying.

"Fence machine is broke." The overseer yanked open the door without knocking. The sun wasn't quite ready to peer over the horizon, but the slave's day began when Old Shaky said it did. "Git to work. Hurry up, boy."

"Yes, suh." Joe's legs were numb from kneeling. "Movin' fast as I can."

"Whippin' take care of your slows."

"Yassuh." Joe let his mouth hang open and adopted the vacant stare of a slave who has to be told three times to do something. If he pretended to have a mouth full of cornmeal mush, he sounded stupid, but when it came to acting ignorant, nobody was better than Marse Williams' inbred son, the one with the big head.

Just how smart is the white man if every one of 'em has a simple son? And how come only the white ones are stupid in the head? Joe started to think: a slave owners' most feared nightmare. *No work involved with waiting,* he thought. *Acting stupid the same as resting.*

"Fencing machine already paid for itself," Old Shaky bragged like he owned it. "But when it ain't drivin' posts, neighbors ain't payin' no money. Get on over to Boone Plantation."

"Boone?" He watched Old Shaky's whip hand. *Ain't even quivered,* he thought. *Wonder how long I can act stupid before he starts shaking? One, two, three ...* Acting stupid was easier than working, and there was a little freedom in each act of rebellion. Everyone rested while Old Shaky was distracted. Joe kept his head steady and his neck rigid but relaxed the muscles that moved his cheeks and eyebrows. He crossed his eyes slightly and kept counting, *eight, nine, ten—*

"You deaf?"

"No suh," he shook his head. *Wonder if I can get all the way up to twenty? Thirteen, fourteen—*

"Goddamn, boy. You was there last week!" When Old Shaky raised his voice, his whip hand got antsy.

"Where?"

"Boone Plantation." Old Shaky's whip hand started to tremble.

"Don't 'member dat, boss." Joe lied, and insurrection bolstered his fledgling courage. *Twenty-three, twenty-four.* "I do recall I turns left."

"Right, Goddammit!"

"Huh. Mos' puzzlesome." *Twenty-eight, twenty—*
Old Shaky uncurled his whip.

"Oh." Joe cocked his head to the side and rubbed his cheek. "Now I 'member." He raised his right hand. "I turns left at the big road."

"Right, God damnit." Old Shaky held up his right hand. "This is right. You turn right." He handed Joe a piece of paper with marks on it. "Got you a pass from the big house. Show this to anybody who stops you."

"Yes suh." He started to back away as soon as Old Shaky let go of the pass. "Right away suh." A blank look of not knowing was a good way to avoid the whip, but being out of reach was better, moving behind a tree, better yet.

Joe turned right when he reached the main road. *This is north!* The grove of trees he and Rachel planned as their first stop, the way the land sloped toward the river, all this was familiar. *Is God showing me the way to freedom? What's beyond all this? Is the river big enough to swim in like we hoped?*

He risked a glance toward all four sides. He was alone on the main road with a pass good for all day. Old Shaky had disappeared into the shack where he kept his still. A stand of shag bark hickory trees hid the big house from view. *Ain't nobody watching me. I can keep on walking past Boone Plantation. Won't nobody know about it till I'm already gone.*

One step, Rachel. One little step. You was right. The next step just got easier.

He left the road and his old life behind, moved the way a deer would, easing forward, each step a gentle transfer of his weight to avoid an unwelcome sound. It was in the ankles, mostly. He twisted his feet one way or the other to avoid stepping on branches or loose rock. Bending his ankle forward allowed him to slide his feet under the leaves and stay quiet. Anyone could move without making noise by practicing patience.

Thank you, Rachel, he thought every time he re-membered to stop and take a long look in all four di-rections. *Getting my own top eye. And it's thanks to you. Don't forget me. Finding my way to you if I got to crawl.*

The stains on his shirt and his pants matched the colors in the ground and the bark on some of the trees. He stayed close to both wherever possible and felt safe enough. He kept seeing a lake off in the distance, but each time he moved toward it, it disappeared.

Is I going crazy?

After two days, his tongue felt too big for his mouth and his throat hurt when he tried to swallow. He moved toward low places, followed the signs water leaves behind. A gentle rain left unevenly spaced clumps of pine needles as it trickled to the bottom of a hill. A hard rain moved fallen trees so the narrow branches pointed the way to a lake. Gully washers formed ditches that cut arrows into the earth. *Every sign of water but none of the real thing.*

"Pow'ful thirsty, Lord," he whispered. "Guide my feet." The sound of his own voice was some comfort. It helped with feeling so alone. He remembered how Rachel taught him to pray.

Best get down on my knees. I know she's waiting, Lord. I still hear her in my dreams like she ain't never left. Please watch over her and Samuel till I get there.

He dusted off his pants and kept walking. Before long, one prayer was answered. He drank his fill from a stream, and then followed it to a river. When a massive log came floating downstream, he swam out to it and held on. He floated until he saw a fire so big the stars overhead were dimmed by light from the flames.

Fire this big, must be an army camp. Problem is, which army?

He let go of the log and swam to the far shore, where a grove of trees reached to the river's edge. He crawled into the forest and hid behind a fallen tree. The river was too wide for him to see what color clothes they wore, but he heard something that made him smile.

> Goodbye hard work with never any pay,
> I'se going up North where the good folks say,
> Gets white bread and a dollar a day,
> Old Shady's coming, coming.
> Hail mighty day.

No black men singing if they slaving for the Rebel army. Got to be Yankees on the other side of this river. He got to his knees and said a prayer of thanks, then swam to the other side.

"Halt!" a sentry shouted. "That's far enough."

"Heard singing," Joe said. He stood in shallow water and raised his hands above his head. "Figured this for a Union camp."

The soldier gave a tight nod. "You figured right. Seen you swimming."

Joe saw a black man who was dressed in a white man's soldiering uniform. There were no holes in his shirt or patches on his pants. He carried a rifle and held it like it belonged to him.

"Lucky you came across to me first," the man said. "Where you from?"

"Don't matter. Ain't going back."

"And your name?"

"Joe."

"Joe what?"

"Just Joe, I guess. Anything but the last name of the white man I run from."

No longer "Joe the slave" from the moment he turned his back to the river and the tobacco plantation, he held out his hands, turned them over, spread his fingers apart.

The hands of a free man. Don't look no different, but I sure ain't never felt more different.

"Where am I?"

"Kentucky. This here's Camp Nelson. That's the Kentucky River you just swum across."

"Thought so. Red pants?" Joe asked, hesitant, looking down at the man's pants. The river water had dried from his own clothes, but they looked even worse next to a soldier's uniform. "Heard something 'bout Union Army giving out red pants."

"Red pants! Huh," the man pointed to the stripes on his uniform sleeve. "See this? Means something better. Mean's sometimes I'm the one giving orders. Look over there." He directed Joe's gaze toward a nearby field.

"They really soldiers?" Men with the same color skin as his wore new blue uniforms. They carried rifles and marched in formation.

A friendlier nod this time. "Their choice. Who you gonna choose to be?"

"Who?" Joe tilted his head to the side and pondered this.

"You your own man, now. What kind of man you gonna be, gonna depend on you."

Well... Joe took a deep breath. *Know where I been. Ain't sure who I can be.* He stretched the kinks out of his back and stood without his head bowed or his shoulders slumped forward. "Figured on fighting—fighting my way to wherever Rachel is."

"Good. Someone be along, soon's the sun come up. Means you got time to decide."

"Decide?"

"That's right. Best choice of all. When I decide to steal myself free, I crosses the Union Lines and throw away my old self: Homer Smith." He snorted in derision. "What kind a white man name is that? I call myself Sengbe Cinque—like the man who led the Amistad revolt." He pointed to the threes stripes sewn onto his sleeve. "Now I'm Private Third Class Sengbe Cinque. Figure on leading my people to freedom, just like the man who stole that ship."

"Ain't heard nothing about that," Joe said. "About all I ever heard is what the white man told me was true."

"That's about to change. Bound to be fighting, soon. No truce flag when we fighting Succesh."

"Succesh?"

"Secede from the Union," Cinque pointed toward the United States flag that flew over the camp headquarters. "That's our flag, now."

"Then it's my flag, too."

"You free to fight back. Maybe the best free of all." Cinque counted off more freedoms on his fingers. "Free to work. Always plenty'a that. Free means you get paid when you work."

"Been paid before. Don't do no good if massa keeps it."

"No massa here. Contrabands, that's you now, gets ten dollars a month minus three for clothes."

"Contraband?"

"What the Yankees calling escaped slaves—the words don't matter so much as the being free. You ain't a slave no more. You free to learn soldiering. Free to go to church. Free to learn reading, free to learn writing "

"Makin marks?" Joe smiled at this. "Like to learn how to mark my name?"

"Free mean a lot of things."

"Just how much free is there?"

"Plenty. Here comes my relief." Cinque snapped to attention and saluted the approaching soldier.

"Suh!" The soldier returned the salute. "You are relieved, suh."

Cinque led Joe past broken wagons and mounds of trash, past a railroad spur and around a ruined depot.

They stopped beside a field where new recruits formed a troop. The men who marched wore shoes. They walked in unison and stayed in step no matter which way they turned. The rising sun glinted off uniform buttons. Their belt buckles flashed when they turned into the sunrise. When they stopped they stood erect, unlike a slave, who was expected to shy away from the master the way a stray dog begs for a handout.

"Act like they ain't afraid of nobody," Joe said in awe. "And they standing so straight!"

"Fear ain't got no place in this fight. Wearing new clothes make it easy to stand up straight, being free make it a habit."

Joe rubbed his fingers against the bandana tied around his neck. The first piece of clothing he'd taken pride in was chewed almost all the way through. He'd slept with the bandanna in his mouth so he wouldn't snore. There wasn't much left of his shirt, either, just dirt and grass stains holding the threadbare cloth together. His pants weren't fit for rags.

"Never seen so many men look like me wearing new clothes." He crossed his arms and held them to his chest, the better to cover his filthy shirt. He could feel the breeze brush against his back where his shirt had torn during a tumble on a rock-strewn hill. His bare feet were so dirty it was hard to tell where his toes stopped and the ground began. Swimming across the river removed a couple of layers of accumulated dirt, but there was enough caked-on mud to hide his toenails. He pointed to his exposed left knee and said, "Everybody I see got new clothes. I got more patch than pant."

That's what Rachel said, he remembered. *'More patch than pant.' I know you listening, Rachel, know we ain't lost what's special between us. Don't give up on me. Won't never give up on you.*

"C'mon. Let's get you settled," Cinque yawned. "Been on duty all night."

Joe nodded but didn't move, just whispered. "They 'bout to start shooting."

The first row of men kneeled and took aim. Their dark blue uniforms stood out the way flowers did in an otherwise barren field. For all the shiny buttons and polished buckles, it was the rifles that drew his gaze. A line of smoke told him they'd fired before the sound of their shots reached his ears. *Never thought of myself as a violent man,* he realized. *But I want to fight. How would it feel to look down the barrel of a Union rifle and see the face of a slaver 'bout to die? Can't imagine. Want to pull a trigger and find out, though.*

Good-natured shouts of encouragement drifted across the field as some targets fell and others remained upright. The acrid smell of gunpowder followed him toward camp. He licked his finger and tested the wind. Staying upwind was the difference between life and death, a habit worth keeping even here, where he felt safe. There were pigs here, chickens and dogs, too. He could smell horses and mules, and the trash mound at the edge of camp. Now that the sun was up, the smell would have been overpowering but for the prevailing winds that blew most of the stench downriver.

More than half of the people he saw were women and children, but their lethargy was gone, the dim-witted façade of enslavement absent. There was uncertainty and fear on some faces, but also hope, and something else he hadn't see much of: people smiling. Children old enough to work were playing instead.

"Supply tent's opening up," Cinque said, moving again. "Let's get you some clothes."

Joe made his mark at the first table, an "X" at the bottom of a piece of paper. A military man wrote "Joe" in the camp book and freedom took a giant step forward.

"What's your last name?"

He looked at his hands. They didn't look different but they belonged to a free man. "I'm a free man."

The man behind the table wrote, "Freeman." He turned the camp register around so Joe could see his name: *Joe Freeman*. "All right?"

"Yes, sir. Joe Freeman." Freedom gave Joe an identity.

The man at the next table sat behind stacks of neatly folded pants. Joe chose a pair of pants without holes or patches. The next table held stacks of shirts he couldn't see through when he held them up for sizing. At each successive table, another item was added to the clothes cradled in his arms. The woman at the last table gave him a personal copy of the Emancipation Proclamation and directed him to the bathhouse.

"Thank you, ma'am." He turned his head to brush away the tears. He left his sorrowful lump of slave clothes on the pile outside the bathhouse.

CHAPTER THIRTEEN

An iron bar blocked Rachel's view. She curled her fingers around the rusted metal and rested her forehead against the window of her jail cell. From her vantage point two stories above Cheapside Street she could watch slaves being auctioned in Lexington's town square. Although it was a rainy, overcast day with sleet falling at times, the street was crowded with people buying, renting, or selling slaves.

"Taking you to the biggest slave auction in the state," Bo had bragged. "Lexington's got the best prices seeing how it's so far from the Ohio River."

Watched people bought and sold for three days… Is this my day to join them?

Rachel ignored their suffering and stared out the window. A clump of stinging nettles grew in the corner of the jail yard where wastewater collected. The spines were painful to touch and most people treated it as a poisonous weed, but Grandma taught her how to use the stinging hairs for pain relief. The barbs worked in reverse and took away pain. The skin above her left ankle was rubbed raw and discolored by rust. The iron shackle around her leg was stained with her blood. Her wounds would heal, the scars would fade, but the hurt went much deeper.

Wish there was something to take away my pain, some herb to cure my memories. Got bruises in the shape of Bo's fingers running up my legs, still got the mark of his boot on my shin where he kicked me. Recognize the smell of his rotted teeth in the sewage overflowing the courtyard and feel his hate in every white man I see, but ain't nobody can hurt me as bad as I hurt myself. Killed my own baby to survive, so I'm gonna survive. I'm tough like that weed.

The uneven trod of footsteps meant the jailer was headed upstairs; he wore heavy boots and walked with a limp. The leg irons he carried clanked together with each step. There were two flights of stairs with thirteen steps each, and he began to wheeze when he neared the second floor. Before he unlocked Rachel's cage, he bent over and put his hands on his knees to catch his breath.

"Turn around," he ordered, and attached a cuff to her right leg. It was damp with someone else's blood.

He locked the second cuff around her left leg before removing the shackle that went around her left ankle and the right ankle of a woman who stared straight ahead and wouldn't speak. "C'mon," the jailer said. "Get your ass downstairs." After a few steps, the new cuff reopened an old wound and Rachel added a layer of her own blood to the dampness with each step down the staircase.

She blinked her eyes against the sunlight streaming through full-length windows facing the sidewalk. A large room at street level was filled with white men wearing suits, but there were women—with straw baskets, and families, too, eating lunch like this was some sort of picnic.

That woman got her blanket spread out in front of a big wood box—looks like oak, about two steps high, two boards wide and five steps long. Why's she sitting there? What's she looking at?

Idle passersby stopped and stared. Sellers and bidders gathered in front of the elevated platform when their lots were called. A fat man dressed in a banker's three-piece suit sat in the corner next to the potbelly stove and used part of the jailer's desk as his branch office.

She overheard the men talking: some slaves were financed, some were sold more than once, and the banker and jailer collected a commission from each seller, buyer, and sometimes, transporter. A slave that sold for one thousand dollars in Louisville might bring five times more money in New Orleans.

Oh God. Is I headed for cotton? Headed for the slow death down south where I'll be worked down to nothing?

"A young mulatto," the auctioneer called out, laying his hand on Rachel's shoulder.

They talking 'bout me! Staring at me, too.

"With child-bearing hips." He refrained from saying whose children, however. The men knew some of the children would be theirs, and their wives pretended not to notice.

Interested buyers moved forward when the auctioneer shoved Rachel up the steps and onto the box. He turned her around so her strong back was visible. Like a horse trainer feeling for heat in a forelock, potential buyers ran their hands along the muscles in her arms and legs. When the price climbed above eight hundred dollars, a potential buyer approached the auction block to inspect her teeth. Most slaves looked older than they were, but teeth didn't lie about age.

The auctioneer lifted her upper lip with his finger. "Got to go higher than eight hundred. Worth a thousand at least. Maybe two. Look here at these teeth. She's young. She—"

Strong teeth. I'll show you strong teeth—bite that finger right off your prying hand.

Bidding stopped when the auctioneer screamed. He yanked his hand away from Rachel's mouth.

Go ahead and cry like a little girl. Rachel spit his severed finger onto the filthy floor beneath her. *You can shake your hand like the pain can't keep up, but it won't do you no good. That stump gonna hurt for a long time and remind you of my sharp teeth you was talking about.*

The promise of profit saved her from a mortal beating, although the jailer needed help to subdue her and drag her upstairs. There would be another auction tomorrow.

Her new cell was an afterthought, designed to hold the overflow of slaves and prisoners awaiting the next day's sale. An accumulation of neglect scrunched beneath her feet, the leftover pile of dirt, wood chips, and unidentifiable litter from periodic sweeping. The jailer was too lazy to pick up the debris, so he swept it into a pile in a corner of the unused cell. The odor of sweat, blood and fear permeated the cell's unfinished wooden walls. Cold air seeped through the gap above her head where a missing shingle illuminated a damp spot on the floor.

Today's prisoners were tomorrow's merchandise and a woman who wouldn't stop praying was shoved into the tiny cell. The jailer secured her ankle to the empty loop attached to Rachel's leg.

"I'll pray for you, child," the woman promised. "Pray to Jesus with me. He gonna hear our prayers."

"He can't hear you from in here; He ain't even listening." Rachel rested her head on her knees and closed her eyes.

"Thank you God," the woman mumbled, "for watching over us. Bless you Jesus, for giving us the strength to keep breathing. We ain't giving up," the woman promised. "Not since you sent someone to stand by our side."

Where are you, Grandma? Asked you to send me a guardian angel, and you sent me a crazy woman who thinks she's talking with God.

"I'm right here, child," the woman said. Her breath carried the familiar scent of pipe tobacco. "I'm holding God's hand and praying right beside you."

Drowsiness lowered Rachel's defenses. Moonlight squeezed through the missing shingle. *Maybe Grandma will visit me in my dreams...*

"I'm right here, child." The woman's voice carried a familiar tone. "You don't recognize me because I'm borrowing the body chained next to you."

Rachel moaned in her sleep.

"Remember all them nights we shared?" Grandma whispered. "Remember the full moon, how we called it a Promise Moon? Look outside. See that same moon? I put it there for you. Your journey ain't done, and I'm still watching over you."

CHAPTER FOURTEEN

Rachel's dream ended with a faint glimmer of hope, but her waking nightmare resumed with the same form of soul murder: slavery. The cell floor smelled and looked like it hadn't been cleaned in months but there was nowhere else to sit. She sat as straight as the shackle allowed and refused to lie down in the filth. The woman beside her stopped praying, but Rachel's longed-for silence remained elusive, for the communal sounds of suffering were no longer held at bay by the rhythmic sounds of prayer. So many ways to cry; all of them present at a slave auction. Each tug on her ankle was a reminder of how far she had fallen, how horrible it was to have company in the depths of her despair.

There was no window in this cell. Denied her last illusion of freedom, she rested her back against the cell wall and looked at what was in front of her. *There's a difference between looking and seeing,* Grandma reminded her.

She stared at her hands. Her fingernails were shiny from the wax the jailer had applied, but all she could see was the dirt under her nails from Samuel's grave. The dried blood on her fingers might have been hers, from the woman who wouldn't stop praying, or from her conscience replaying Samuel's dying spasms and the blood that foamed from his lungs. Despite the nightmares and guilt, these tainted hands with their morbid history were the hands of a healer.

Although a shackle encircled her ankle, her hands were free. Sassafras root for stomach ache or slippery elm bark for pain relief, Grandma taught her about medicinal roots and healing herbs, but she also showed her how to tend to the sick with what little was available.

More healing in knowing a person care, Grandma always said. *Caring more powerful than tonic.* Grandma was gone, but her gentle spirit remained. Rachel could still hear her next words as clearly as the day she said them: *I pray you get free, child. Only soul comfort there is.*

She couldn't remember what it was like to be comforted, for she and Joe had been apart for months. She dreaded another person's touch, but she reached out to comfort the woman who wouldn't stop praying. It was what Grandma would have done.

"God be praised," the woman chained to Rachel's ankle said. "He brought you back from nearly dead. A couple times last night you stopped breathing, but Jesus reached down into this cell and touched your soul. You all the proof I need that God's listening."

Rachel put her arm around the woman's shoulder.

"Pray with me, child. It's twice as strong when we both praying."

Rachel pulled her knees up to her chest and bent her head. She closed her eyes but no prayers would come.

"Where there despair, bring some hope," the woman prayed.

If I could bring myself to pray, might pray for revenge. But ain't no point praying to a God who's abandoned me.

"Where there weakness, bring us some strength. Where there darkness ..." the woman faltered. She took a deep breath but the words left her. A low moan eased aside her belief, tears formed in place of faith. She bowed her head, but her grief was too severe for silence. She began to sob. Each spasm traveled the length of her body and passed through the shackle around her ankle.

Rachel couldn't find a comfortable place to rest her arm around the woman's shoulders. She didn't let that stop her. If helping others was what it took to get through heartbreak, then she would do it.

Staying to myself is the worst form of not living. Had enough pain from missing Joe, but I can't seem to do nothing about that. Pain just comes. Time for me to do what Grandma taught me: help others.

"Dry your tears," she whispered, and pulled the woman close. "Lean up against me."

"I'm all prayed out."

"I know." Rachel hugged the woman's shoulders. "I'll pray for both of us. I'll pray for grace."

The woman turned and leaned her forehead against Rachel's arm, her warm tears fell onto Rachel's skin. Grief flowed through them and joined the collective suffering of a crowded jail for the enslaved. Muffled sobs and muted weeping slipped through the barred windows and locked gates—the evening sounds of a prison at the close of another business day, with nothing but the silent prayers of those suffering to lessen the pain.

The woman fell asleep and started to snore. Despite the discomfort of the added weight against her shoulder, Rachel fell asleep, too. The dream world used the woman's sonorous bass notes to mimic the sound of the ocean. Storm waves boomed against the hull of a slave ship in tempo with her breathing. The evening mist crept beneath the cell door and wrapped Rachel's dream ship in fog. It was warm in this crowded jail and the air flowing through the missing shingle carried far-off sounds that defied understanding. A peculiar rattle, rhythmic clinks, perhaps the shuffling of feet, this was the language of dreams...

A woman who favored Grandma was chained in the hold of a slave ship. She had the same small ears tucked close to the sides of her head like Rachel and her mama. A pronounced chin gave her cheekbones an angular slant rising toward the far corners of her eyes and imparted an unusual symmetry to her facial features. It was Grandma's mother but no one knew her name.

The cargo hold was cramped and dark. Three-foot ceilings had small slits cut into the floors and provided inadequate ventilation. Large jars sat in the corner of each hold for a privy, but they were impossible for her to reach because the woman chained to her was dead. The slaves above and below suffered equally. Women gave birth and people died; a child drowned in one of the large jars. Some captives jumped off board with maniacal laughter, singing as the sharks dragged them under water. Some slaves starved themselves, hoping for death, but Grandma's mother was a survivor. She endured the middle passage. She reached from beyond understanding to remind Rachel of an infinite truth.

I survived a boat ride across the ocean, child, means you can survive anything, too. This is what I passed on to you: the will to live, the pride in not giving up.

The man waited outside the jail until the street was deserted. There was dust on his clothes from traveling. He held a wad of cash in his pocket, and hoped it would be enough for the slave he wanted; it was all he could steal.

He waited for the last man to leave before he crossed the street and opened the lobby door. He didn't step fully inside. His scowl was of a man who didn't like what he saw. It was critical he didn't appear eager. That would drive up the price, and he couldn't afford to make a mistake. He wrinkled his nose against the stench of fear and filth, tilted his head to the side and let his eyelids slide partway down until they began to block his vision, affecting disinterest. "Might be interested in some of your stock," he said.

"You? We sell your kind in here. Get your ass outta here boy, if you don't want to be next."

"I'm a free man, an' I got the papers to prove it." *And Lord, if you're listening, send an angel to make sure this white man don't ask for proof.*

"Don't get uppity with me, boy."

"I got cash—white man's money." He remained in the doorway. "More money than that high-tempered bitch is worth."

"You? Why you wanting to buy one of your own kind?"

"Ain't the only black man to own slaves. Ain't the only man needing a wife, neither. Besides, I got money. White-man's money."

The manager blinked and looked away, put his hands on his lap to shield his bandaged stump. "She's spirited, that's all."

"Maybe. Or maybe she'll stab me first chance she gets." The black man approached the side of the desk the banker was using earlier and carefully placed a greenback onto the surface. "Like I said. White-man's money." He peeled another greenback from the wad of money, snapped it straight before carefully placing it on top of the previous one. By surreptitiously putting a small crease in the underside of each banknote, the pile appeared taller than the bills forming it were worth. He stopped when the stack threatened to tip over.

"She's young," the manager said. "Pretty, too. Got child-bearing hips, just the—"

"How's your finger?"

It took the business manager several seconds before he could look away from the stack. "Keep going," he croaked.

The would-be buyer moved around to the front of the desk instead, leaned over and stared at the man's hand. "Best get a doctor to look at that finger. Before it rots and falls off."

"She'll clean up real nice," the manager cleared his throat. "She's something special, knew it that the first time I seen her."

"She's trouble, and you know it." Slowly, he held another greenback up to the light and snapped it. "Word gets out about that finger—next time she's up on the block, won't bring but half what you're asking, maybe less." Ever so gently, he laid another new bill on top of the existing pile. When the pile was about an inch taller, he put his hands in his pockets. "I'm willing to take a chance. Are you?"

From the manager's lips came a muffled, "Hmm."

The man reached for the stack of money and started to slide it off the desk.

"Wait a minute." The manager slapped his left hand, the one with all its fingers, on top of the money.

"Too late." He slid the bills out from beneath the manager's hand.

"Not so fast. Lemme see that cash again."

"Not without a bill of sale."

"She's young."

"With sharp teeth. Taking a risk as it is." He casually flicked his wrist and sent the money flying onto the desk. One of the bills fluttered to the floor.

"All right. Sold. And you're welcome to her." The business manager used the finger on his unbitten hand to summon the jailer. "Bring her down. And be quick about it."

The jailer trudged up the stairs with a whip in one hand and a heavy iron key in the other. The slaves on the second floor grew quiet at the sound of footsteps, knowing nothing good came up those steps. He reached through the bars and removed the shackle from Rachel's ankle. "Shut the hell up," he told the other woman when she started praying.

A week's worth of bruises still ached, and Rachel's bloody ankle made it painful to walk. Going down the first few stairs reopened the wound. She paused to keep from falling when the pain began.

"Keep moving." He prodded her in the back with the butt of his whip.

She made it halfway down the stairs, but froze at what awaited her in the lobby. Her mind reeled at the treachery.

"Outside, bitch," the manager growled at her. "You too, boy." He glared at the black man and jerked his head in the direction of the door.

When Rachel didn't move, the business manager stomped up the stairs to where she stood. He grabbed her upper arm and dragged her toward the door, but wisely kept his fingers away from her mouth.

The jailer took a step forward, whip in hand, but the black man shook his head. "Got my own whip and my carriage is around the corner, I'll get her there." He grabbed her arm and yelled, "Goddamn it to hell, bitch. C'mon!"

Rachel tried to jerk her arm free of his grasp but failed. The man leaned toward her as he yanked her arm again, and whispered, "Keep fighting. It's our only chance."

Once they were outside, he turned and headed for the opposite corner. She stumbled to keep up. In response, he yanked her arm and muttered, "They might come outside to watch us. Keep struggling."

"Don't know why," she whispered back. "Deacon Turner, you wouldn't know how to hurt a flea." She kept struggling, though, but not enough to slow them down. He didn't let go of her until they were out of sight around the corner.

He twisted her arm behind her back in case anyone was watching and forced her into a carriage.

"Where'd you get this?"

"Stole it, after I sold my wagon and mules to get enough money to buy you free." He pulled on the reins and turned the carriage toward the north.

CHAPTER FIFTEEN

Rachel and Deacon Turner followed buffalo traces instead of rivers and traveled at night. Cloudy skies hid the North Star, but the sun set in the west, so they kept their left shoulders pointed toward the western horizon and traveled north. They had to abandon the wagon when a winter storm swept down from Canada and dropped enough snow to turn everything white. Gusting winds formed chest-high drifts, so they took turns forging a narrow passageway through the snow and proceeded on foot until they lost their way.

"Rivers flow to the south," she assured him. They followed the contours of the land as it sloped downhill toward a river. "All we got to do is throw a stick in the water and see which way it floats. Downstream is south, so we'll just turn our backs to that stick and keep on to the North."

The river was frozen.

"Afraid if I sit down long enough to rest—won't never get up." Deacon Turner braced his hands against his knees. His back was bowed and his head hung below his shoulders from exhaustion. "There's more storm coming. Feel it in the bump on my leg bone where a mule kicked me."

"Think you're right," Rachel said. "Birds are roosting low in the trees. Haven't seen any animal tracks for hours, must mean they're gonna wait out the coming storm."

"Think we'd better do the same." Ice crystals dotted his beard and moustache. "Need to find some kind of shelter. Don't think I got another night of sleeping outdoors left in me."

"We'll follow the river. If there's any shelter around here, it's bound to be near water."

He pushed off against his knees and slowly stretched the kinks out of his back. He rubbed his eyes and slowly turned in a circle. "How we gonna tell which way's north?"

Rachel pressed the tips of her fingers against her thumbs, closed her eyes and concentrated on feeling her heartbeat. When she could follow her pulse all the way down her arms and feel the tingle in her fingers, she let her top eye wander. It wasn't magic. She paid attention to her surroundings. She turned into the wind. "Storm like this, it's got to be coming all the way from Canady. Think heading into the wind is north."

Deacon Turner followed Rachel's example. He closed his eyes and took deep breaths through his nose to test the air. "Think I smell smoke." Rounding the next bend in the river, he recognized the distinctive aroma of a smokehouse. "Smells like meat curing. Ham, bacon, maybe some beef, too—smoking under a hickory wood fire and sweetened with just a touch of honey. It's got me to remembering how hungry I am."

"Warm and smoky is better than freezing to death," Rachel whispered. They were crouched behind a stand of holly bushes weighed down by deep red berries. A house on the opposite side of the river belonged to a rich person. It had a private dock and more rooms than days of the month. Tendrils of smoke curled away from a tiny, square brick house with a witch's key set near the roof.

"That keyhole made from missing bricks is to let the evil spirits out," Deacon Turner said. "Don't want to take no chances when it comes to curing meat."

"Don't want to take no chances getting caught, neither. Won't take long for the storm to reach us. We'll wait until it starts snowing," Rachel said. "That way nobody will see us cross over the ice and the snow-flakes will cover our tracks—I hope."

⟞⊷ ⊶⟝

Rachel and Deacon Turner sat on the edge of a brine trough and ate smoked ham cured with hickory wood. The smokehouse walls were covered with soot, and soon, so were their clothes, but wool dries from the inside first. Once they warmed up, they'd stay that way. It was warm by the smoldering fire but too smoky to breathe without coughing. They took turns warming up by the fire or crouched near the entrance, sucking at the trickle of fresh air that snuck beneath the door. Grandma watched over both of them when they fell asleep. The wind shifted direction and blew a steady stream of fresh air beneath the door. The cook inside the rich person's house decided on chicken for dinner and stayed out of the smokehouse. The fire smoldered all night and it stayed warm inside.

Early the next morning, a cowbell clanked nearby and announced the return of daylight. A dog barked, but it was the sound of a pet, not a bloodhound. Rachel eased the door open far enough to look both ways. The storm had become a blizzard but it wasn't safe to stay inside the smokehouse any longer.

The brutal cold kept the rivers iced over for six days, so Rachel and Deacon Turner stayed close to the shore where the ice was frozen solid enough to walk on. They found a river that meandered north. It took two nights of walking before they learned they were following the Licking River—named for the salt licks that form on its banks. Four more nights of walking and they realized they were following the curviest river in the state.

"At least there ain't many people," Deacon Turner said.

"And we're going north, generally. Keep hoping the next curve is the last one." Rachel had developed a cough that steadily grew worse. The coughing fits got so bad they carried blood, and every time she wiped the blood off her palms she was reminded of Samuel's death. "Best keep moving. Afraid if I stand in one place too long, might turn into a block of ice—won't be able to move till the thaw."

Deacon Turner had lost the feeling in most of his toes and walked with a limp. His fingers were turning blue and starting to feel like his toes did before the dull ache of frostbite took away his natural step. He tested the air for smoke. He knew hiding in smoke-houses made Rachel's cough worse, but these small buildings were the only warm place to hide where there weren't any people. The aroma of smoked meat meant the small houses were the easiest places to find. "Sure ain't gonna die hungry, but afraid if we don't reach the Ohio River before thaw, won't be no way to get across."

"Fears might come true but dreams don't die unless you let them. Ain't giving up. Grandma wouldn't like it." Rachel took another step north and kept moving toward freedom. "Reckon the unexpected is what's gonna happen next."

The bounty hunters and pattyrollers emerged from indoors when the storm passed after six days of freezing weather. Union Army reinforcements arrived with the thaw, but the soldiers were too busy chasing Confederate soldiers from the northern reaches of the state during daylight to help escaped slaves at night. When Rachel and Deacon Turner reached the Ohio River, they prayed for another blizzard. Maybe God heard their prayers but had a better answer than more bad weather. Maybe it was Grandma watching over them, since help appeared in the least likely way.

"Don't trust nobody but got to have help from somebody." Deacon Turner had his shoes off and was trying to massage some life into his toes with unfeeling fingers. He kept his lips close to Rachel's ear so his whispers wouldn't be overheard. "That light up on top of the highest hill on the free side got to be some kind of signal. Chopped on enough trees to know that nobody burns that much wood for no reason."

Been hearing someone pounding on the free side of the river for three nights straight. Rachel couldn't speak and suppress a coughing fit at the same time, but she could nod her head in agreement.

"That light and all that noise got to be some kind of signal," Deacon Turner said. "Ain't no coincidence the pattyrollers and Yankee soldiers get all riled up on the slaving side of the river whenever there's a bonfire or some kind of pounding going on over at the free side."

Rachel nodded. When the coughing spasms went this deep, the episode was nearly over. She uncovered her mouth when the coughing spell passed but knew better than to look at her palm. *More blood on my hands, just adding to the stain that's already there from killing Samuel.* She wiped her palm on the ground instead of adding to the blackened bloodstain on her clothes left behind from previous fits.

"Think I hear something." Deacon Turner's breath against her ear formed the only warm spot on her body. "Thinking it was just a big fish but the splashes is too regular."

"Thinking the same thing, then remembering the sound of Hercules rowing a leaky boat. Sounds almost the same. But now I ain't so—"

"What is it?"

"Dawgs." She eased aside the top branches of a spindly juniper bush. This stunted evergreen was the last available place to hide in the sparsely vegetated strip of land between the river and forest. The torches were close enough for her to see the yellowish-orange of the flames and the pale faces of the three bounty hunters holding them aloft, but the dogs were closer. She cringed when their howls changed to the excited yips of bloodhounds closing in on their prey. Her mouth went dry except for the bitter taste of fear, she couldn't remember ever being this scared, but nothing felt worse than her first step into the frigid waters of the Ohio River.

Deacon Turner gasped. "Hell must be cold." He reached for her hand.

Rachel clasped his hand and intertwined her fingers with his. Her body tensed against the cold until she could feel the ache in her muscles.

"There's that splashing again." A violent shiver shook Deacon Turner hard enough to make a splash of his own. "Reckon that's Satan come for my soul. Never thought of him as a big fish, though."

"That ain't no fish. My mind's playing tricks on me, hearing things that ain't there—but I swear it sounds like Hercules is rowing across the river, coming to save us."

They waded into the river when the dogs emerged from the edge of the forest. Rachel stopped when the water was waist-high and the strong current nearly swept her off her feet.

"Now I'm seeing things." She put a hand on Deacon Turner's shoulder for balance. "There's a boat." She pointed toward the middle of the river.

"Or a big chunk of ice." He leaned forward and squinted. "Ain't ruling out a big fish, neither. Don't matter, though. We ain't got no choice but to swim out there and hang on."

"Or die trying." Rachel took a deep breath and let go of his hand. She plunged into the freezing water of the Ohio River and started swimming.

Rachel swam toward a boat, but it was Grandma swirling the water to send a message of hope. Deacon Turner started swimming when he heard the dogs splash into the water. The dogs howled from the cold and returned to shore. Rachel heard the bounty hunters curse at the dogs for turning back, heard the dogs yelp with pain when the men forced them back into the water with their torches. The flames cast a yellowish light and turned the water an oily shade of gray. She heard a muted splash from muffled oars and altered her course, but it was an uprooted tree caught in the deadly currents of the Ohio River. A tree branch struck her in the shoulder. She raised her arm to ward off the next blow and her sleeve snagged on one of the broken limbs. A vortex spun the entire tree in a circle and the roots knocked Deacon Turner underwater.

Rachel yanked at her sleeve. She yanked again and the worn fabric pulled loose at the seam. She lowered her shoulder and ducked beneath the log to shed the tangled cloth, but the current spun her away from the tree and toward deeper water. The river swept against her waterlogged shoes and loose pants, dragging her toward the depths of the main channel. The turbulent water disoriented her and she was too far underwater to see the surface. *Hell's gonna be wet and cold, and I'm almost there.*

Grandma reached up from the bottom of the river and tickled Rachel's feet until she bent her knees and furiously kicked her legs. When Grandma touched Rachel's ticklish sides, she bent her elbows and frantically swept her arms. Kicking her legs and flailing her arms, Rachel reoriented herself and accelerated toward the surface. She bumped her head against some unrecognizable debris but it yielded to her momentum and she burst above the surface, dragging the debris with her.

"Thought you was a fish," Deacon Turner gasped.

"Figured you for a log—wait, think I see one coming."

"Strange looking log, but there ain't nothing else around here to hold on to." He started swimming.

Freezing water nearly killed them, but a big chunk of frozen water saved them. Maybe God has a sense of humor, or perhaps it was Grandma, up in heaven showing the Angels how to make do with what they had instead of having what they wanted. Grandma used what the Ohio River gave her, an ice floe big enough for two people to crawl onto.

"Ain't complaining, mind you," Deacon Turner said, "but a big chunk of ice about the last thing I was hoping for."

Rachel nodded. Another coughing spell had grabbed her and wouldn't let go long enough for her to speak.

1864

CHAPTER SIXTEEN

Rachel and Deacon Turner survived. The northern bank of the Ohio River was where "The North" began. They joined the poorest of the poor living in a contraband camp on the periphery of Cincinnati, Ohio, and downwind of the Union Army's trash dump at Camp Dennison. Picked-over, unwanted items were salvaged and reused in the camp. Wood turning to dust from termite infestation formed the walls of shacks, rusted-through tin or scrap metal served as a roof. Rags and paper were wedged into the cracks in an unsuccessful effort to slow the cold seeping through the makeshift chinking, and the people inside huddled around uncertain flames. The smoke from their meager fires reeked of garbage and tainted the clothing of anyone who visited and all who lived there. This was their haven. As bad as conditions were, slavery was worse. No freed slave willingly returned to enslavement.

The simple grey woolen dress, the navy-blue linsey-woolsey blouse with plain wooden buttons, and the sturdy, square-toed black shoes Rachel wore were compliments of the Cincinnati African Methodist Episcopal (AME) congregation. There was a shelter in the basement and she volunteered in the clinic that tended to the sick. When members of the congregation stood to join the choir in song, she tucked her hands behind her back and shared a hymnal with the lady next to her.

> *"Free at last, free at last,*
> *I thank God I'm free at last.*
> *On my knees when the light passed by,*
> *I thank God I'm free at last.*
> *Thought my soul would rise and fly,*
> *I thank God I'm free at last."*

Deacon Turner carried a collection plate and started up the aisle. He walked with a permanent limp from losing his toes. His pockets were turned inside out as a way of demonstrating he had nothing left to give. There were already rumors that he kept most of his money in his shoes but Rachel didn't gossip. She knew there wasn't much profit in selling fruits and vegetables or hauling corpses.

Rachel didn't have any money to give, so she kept her hands folded in her lap. She couldn't look at her hands without seeing their lethal past and kept them hidden beneath a shawl.

Let Joe find the courage to get free. And give him the gift of forgiveness if he learns I killed our child rather than let myself get caught.

Deacon Turner made friends easily. He remembered names. He listened more than he talked, so people just naturally stopped to visit with him before leaving.

"Mrs. Smith's children got the pox."

"There's hay for sale near the Whitewater Canal Tunnel. Oats, too."

"They say Yellow Fever killing more Succesh than Union bullets."

"Found two bodies from the fire this week. They was under all the rubble."

A neighborhood boarding house burned to the ground three days ago—arson. The white fire department hadn't bothered to respond, although some of the volunteer firemen joined the white people watching and cheering as the building burned.

Deacon Turner gathered the last of the news and barred the front doors. He descended the flight of stairs leading to the basement, where half windows at ground level provided light and white paint covered the unadorned walls to make the most of the indirect lighting. A stove in the far corner provided heat in the winter and meals for whomever was hungry. Folded cots lined the walls. It was too cold to play outside, so the children played in a corner made possible by pushing the tables aside. A patchwork quilt in a double diamond pattern covered one of the tables near the windows.

"Sure feels good to sit down—even if only for a little while." There was a touch of sandpaper in the rough edges of Deacon Turner's voice. He poured a glass of lukewarm lemonade from a pitcher sitting on the table. The cooks boiled the water every morning so it would be safe to drink.

"Heard about a job opening up," the woman next to Rachel whispered. Somerset Clay Wilson Speed Stone kept each owner's last name in hopes of one day finding her family. Introductions took longer with Somerset, but she was determined to find at least one living relative. "The ancestors want to be remembered," Somerset told everyone she met. "I feel it in my dreams, know it in my heart." She held a needle up to the light so she could rethread it.

"I'll never forget Grandma." Rachel worked on the quilt's border. Her strong fingers could push a needle through the extra layers of cloth.

"Starting a sewing circle one of the best things we ever did." Somerset would get a ride to the Cincinnati Marine Hospital when it was time for her shift to start.

"Heard you already got this quilt sold," Deacon Turner said. He offered transportation to the women who volunteered in the sewing circle.

Each quilt carried a piece of Rachel's sorrow, quietly shared in the confidence of a sewing circle where differences were temporarily put aside for communal benefit. Every square she sewed became a repository of grief, yet each quilt also carried hope; hope that money from the sale would help more of their people break free. The finished quilts carried a piece of each woman's story, told in the safety of a gathering devoted to helping others escape the pain every woman shared.

"This reminds me a little of brush arbor gatherings," Somerset recalled. "Only we sewing on a quilt instead of sitting around a pot full of water."

"Never heard of brush arbor gatherings," Rachel said. "Go on about it."

"Water pot hides our voices." Somerset said. "When pain got too great, we went to the brush arbor where it was safe to talk the truth."

"Everybody know it's safe to talk truth in the sewing circle." The women leaned forward when Mrs. Smith spoke. It grew more difficult to hear her as winter progressed and the cold turned her raspy voice into a hoarse whisper. She had lost most of her voice from years spent breathing dust while fanning rice. Freedom cost Mrs. Smith her husband. Somerset had lost all of her family. Deacon Turner was missing most of his toes. Rachel had developed a cough that wouldn't quit, but she covered her mouth with a handkerchief and hid the blood between the folds.

"Something about saying the truth lessens the pain," Somerset said. "True then; true now." She sorted through the spools of thread until she found one in a dark shade of green. "Maybe talking truth makes a little room for hope."

"Hope in these quilts," Mrs. Smith said. "Each square I sew takes away a little pain."

"Quilts bring money and that buys freedom." Somerset expertly tied two knots together so the thread would hold. She bit off the loose ends. "More hope in being free than anything else."

"All my slave days, I hear promises about going to heaven in a chariot instead of walking. Hear about wearing golden robes 'stead of rags." Mrs. Smith sorted through the material scraps for a new square. "Got tired of waiting for promises that never come."

"Most of my promises already broke—except for waiting on Joe," Rachel confessed.

"We're all praying for him." Mrs. Smith picked up a square of blue paisley that had once been a scarf and held it in place to see the effect.

"God sure to hear one of us." Rachel handed Mrs. Smith the newly threaded needle. On the days when Mrs. Smith's hands shook too hard to thread a needle, she sewed backings on the squares so the shaky stitches didn't show. She rested her hands on the table, slowing the tremors. This way she could sew by moving the material instead of the needle.

"No place is home without Joe." Rachel pinned the square of blue paisley in place and Mrs. Smith began to sew.

"First loss always seem hardest. Maybe it's not being used to the pain." Mrs. Smith's voice was hoarse and difficult to hear. The agony from knowing such profound loss raised the bass notes in her raspy tone an octave. "When that's gone, pain just keep coming." When the tremors became too severe to sew, Mrs. Smith intertwined her fingers and placed her hands in her lap.

"Losing children the hardest loss of all," Somerset said.

Rachel looked away, lest her own hands betray her. She moved her chair closer to the table to hide her hands beneath the quilt.

"Cost of running always more than we're willing to pay." Mrs. Smith leaned forward until her upper arms rested against the table. "Cost of staying is worse."

"Only the Devil strike a bargain like that," Somerset said. "Devil got his hand in slavery and don't want to let go."

"Used to think learning I was a slave was the worst until I learned I was a slave woman." Rachel paused from her sewing. All she had to do was close her eyes to see Joe. "Leaving Joe behind was when the troubles start piling up and the pain never stop." Her memory of killing Samuel haunted her at night when she was alone with her guilt.

"So much pain." Mrs. Smith's tremors passed and she resumed sewing. "Hope the worst pain is behind."

"Hope my children in heaven." Somerset looked away when the tears dropped onto the fabric.

Mrs. Smith reached out to comfort her. They might fuss like sisters, but they sat so close together their chairs were touching.

"Each quilt different, but each quilt seems to carry away little bit of my pain," Mrs. Smith said. "Must mean it freeing somebody. Some hope in that."

"If it helps Joe get free, then it's the best quilt of all." Rachel tied her last knot and put her hands behind her back. *What am I gonna do about these bloody hands? You taught me how to heal others, Grandma, but how am I gonna heal myself? What kind of herb can cure me of seeing my baby's blood on my hands?*

It was time for her to leave. Despite the bloodstains, these were the hands of a healer. With Deacon Turner's help, she could bring a small measure of comfort to her fellow refugees in the Contraband Camp—the poorest of the poor.

Deacon Turner's wagon was parked in the alley behind the church. He didn't need a whip, couldn't bear to use one on any living creature after having been whipped, himself. The mules were trained to work and taken care of when they did. Their hooves slid off rounded cobblestones made slick by a light rain. They were sure-footed, however, and managed a foothold in the spaces between the rocks. Deacon Turner always parked his wagon facing downhill. The scraping-and-sliding sound of hooves lessened. After a few false starts, the clattering of wooden wheels bouncing between uneven cobblestones echoed off brick buildings.

"Got these blankets from the Cincinnati Marine Hospital," Rachel said. "Found them in the alley between Sixth and Lock streets. Every dead soldier leaves at least one blanket behind and they was throwing all of them out." She shook her head at such waste.

"Better than the carpet scraps they using at Camp Dennison." Deacon Turner glanced over his shoulder at the bundle resting in the back of his wagon. "Those blankets a strange shade of blue. Halfway between storm-brewing sky blue and downright black."

"Some of them was worn, maybe a hole or two. Some of them was stained, but I boiled them with sunflower seeds. Found some cabbage and a little cherry tree root, so I added that, too. All I could get on short notice."

"Won't matter to somebody who's been cold for months. Long as they're keeping a body warm, don't guess nobody'll complain." Deacon Turner flicked the reins to get the mules' attention. "Easier going around the block than fighting our way up it. We'll turn at the next street. Work our way back to the camp." He pulled some slack from the reins and gently guided the mules along a path they were already familiar with.

"Thought maybe some of the women could turn the extras into pants."

"I've worn worse. More patch than pant."

"Seen the same on Joe." *What I wouldn't give to see Joe again. Even if he's still wearing those raggity old pants.*

The mules knew to stop beside the butcher's shop on 4th street. The butcher owned the building and lived on the second floor above the shop with his wife, two sons and a daughter. Vegetable gardens grew on every available piece of unoccupied soil. A man who can eat meat is rich in an alley community subsisting largely on cornmeal and vegetables. His wife wore a Sunday dress of broadcloth and crinoline and his children attended school. He could afford to donate soup bones, scraps and meat too old to sell.

The next stop was for water. Surreptitiously, Deacon Turner reached into his shoe for payment. He rolled empty casks off the wagon and secured replacements full of potable water in their place.

The milliner on Water Street made plain, sturdy hats from castoff cloth. They weren't much to look at, but the broad brims kept the sun off people's faces. Women who worked in the camp's vegetable gardens and men who worked outdoors wore these simple hats. They didn't complain about the lack of style, grateful to have their faces shielded from the sun. Bruised fruit at the produce market, stale bread at the bakery on Front Street, the wagon was filled with goods until there was nothing left in either shoe.

"Seem like you always got plenty to give," Rachel said. "Been meaning to ask you about that."

"Some prayers get answered. Nothing against the church, but I figure they got it backwards. Been giving away ninety percent and keeping the tithe for myself. Ain't never wanted for nothing. You and me know all the money in the world can't buy what's priceless. Can't buy freedom. That was something you and me stole for ourselves."

The mules moved faster but pulled easier as they moved downhill. The trend was downward as well. Living conditions steadily deteriorated as they approached the camp. Hovels and makeshift packing-crate huts dotted the alleys, A peculiar stench hovered above this part of the Ohio River that would remain in their clothes until the next laundering.

"These flies is thick." Deacon Turner gripped the reins with one hand and waved away flies with the other. Clouds of black flies shifted from one side of the river to the other along with the breeze. A strong wind brought temporary relief from their incessant droning but they always managed to find their way back to the Contraband camps that had formed on the fringes of the military strongholds at Camp Dennison and Camp Clay.

Rachel stared at old, condemned hospital tents arranged in rows parallel to the river, their canvas so rotten, guy ropes wouldn't hold in high winds. But there was life here, and nowhere more evident than in the faces of the delighted children who ran to greet them. Because of the butcher and baker they would be fed. Because of Rachel they might be healed. Through the generosity of Deacon Turner, who donated the use of his wagon and the money he made from hauling goods, all this was possible.

Children surrounded her. Mothers carrying infants approached, an uncomfortable reminder of her loss. From the newspaper read at each church service, she'd learned that dysentery, diarrhea, typhoid and malaria took the lives of 10 percent of the Union soldiers and 20 percent of the men in the Confederate Army. The disease rate was higher in contraband camps. She treated children who suffered from measles, mumps, chickenpox and whooping cough, giving out belladonna for fever and yellow jasmine for headaches. Raw onion and garlic juice mixed with honey helped children stop coughing. Nothing seemed to cure her persistent cough, but she didn't complain. *Just another cost of freedom.*

A mother walked up to her clutching her baby, both wracked by coughing. The baby held up his arms like Samuel used to when he was feeling cranky. Rachel tossed him in the air until he giggled. She held her tears for later and repeated her prayer for Joe to steal himself free.

And when he gets free, give him a way to forgive me for killing our child because I can't forgive myself...

CHAPTER SEVENTEEN

The boarding house was five blocks from the church, which is how Rachel was first to apply for the job ahead of the twenty or so applicants that arrived throughout the rest of the day. She raised her hand to knock on the door and her gaze settled on her ring finger, at the simple band on her left hand. She hadn't seen Joe for more than a year but it felt like a century. He hadn't given the ring to her; she made it herself from discarded wire. The inside of the band turned her finger green but it was priceless as a symbol of their vows to each other, and sometimes it allowed her to look at her hands without seeing the bloodstains. Each time she looked at the ring, it helped change her mind about leaving before Joe joined her. She no longer allowed herself to dream of Canada. No place felt like home without Joe. No matter how much she longed to run again, she prayed that one day Joe would find the courage to escape.

Miss Antoinette Hall owned the nicest boarding house in Cincinnati, Ohio. *Lust, greed* and *envy, sloth* and *anger, pride* and *gluttony,* she wore the seven deadly sins engraved on a locket that never left her neck, the edges worn smooth from the habitual caress of fingertips. A petite woman with dangerous curves and flawless skin that men begged to touch, in this era of pale, fragile beauty she made other women appear anemic and malnourished. Her grayish-green eyes picked up the color of whatever clothing she wore, and men who looked once seldom looked away. Miss Antoinette glanced at Rachel's hands and saw the chipped nails of a scrubwoman, the scratched and swollen fingers of a maid.

"Maybe you'll do," she said. "Follow me."

"Yes, ma'am," Rachel put her hands behind her back. The job didn't pay much, maid work, but came with a place to sleep.

Soot coated the ornate brass fixtures in the hallway and the smudged glass cast irregular shadows. Dust softened the outlines of lions carved into the staircase railings. Scuffmarks defaced the baseboards. The carpets were dirty.

"This is my room." It took two keys to unlock Miss Antoinette's door. "Pick these up." She pointed to the dirty clothes piled on the floor. "And be quick about it."

"Yes, ma'am."

The dressing screen, the room divider, even the closet doors partially hiding a safe had a painting on them. A marble mantle above the fireplace held the fancy kind of breakables rich people collected. Delicate blue cups and saucers covered the mantle and filled a corner cupboard. Chubby white babies with wings covered the ceiling. A long bathtub rested on cast-iron animal claws and reminded her of the soldiers with amputated legs who hobbled around on crutches.

"Go on, get out." Miss Hall dismissed Rachel with an abrupt wave of her hand. "And bring me my bathwater."

"Yes, ma'am." Rachel backed out of the room and Miss Hall slammed the door in her face. The first lock clicked into place, but the second lock slid shut with the sound of a well-oiled rifle bolt. "Good Lord," she sighed. "What have I got myself into?"

Dirty linen lay in untidy bundles beside each upstairs bedroom door, a zigzag pathway of rumpled sheets stretched the length of the hallway. She picked up as many mounds of bedclothes as she could carry and took the bundle downstairs, then out to the alley. The kitchen occupied a small brick building thirteen steps from the back door of the house. Too decrepit for slave quarters, the crumbling building was adequate for hired help.

She added wood to the softly glowing coals nestled in the firebox and breathed new life into the stove since Miss Antoinette's garish tub held a stovetop of hot water. When she carried the last bucket of bathwater to Miss Antoinette's room and raised her hand to knock on the door, careful habits stopped her fist halfway through the first downward swing. The memory of her grandmother came with a warning.

Use your top eye, child. Look for what ain't supposed to be there. Listen for what don't belong.

She unclenched her fist and pressed her palm against the door, put her ear next to it. Tumblers dropping into place with mechanical *thunks* penetrated the door as bass notes amid the treble tones of a spinning dial. The safe opened with the double click of a shotgun being readied to fire. She waited for an end to the sound of tumblers spinning. When the vault-like sound of a safe door closing entered the hallway, she knocked and called out. "Rest of your bathwater, ma'am."

Miss Antoinette opened the door and motioned her inside. There was no mud or manure on this carpet, just rugs on top of rugs, each with fringe on the edges and swirls of color so deep, the patterns seemed to go all the way through to the floor. The rugs were thick and her feet sank with each silent step, the way they did when walking barefoot on a fresh-cut lawn.

"Go on, pour that water, then get out." Miss Antoinette added scented oil to the bathwater and checked the temperature with her little finger. "And bring more hot water!"

Rachel exhaled when the door closed behind her. *This a room for trouble in a troubled house. Best watch my step.*

About the time she shifted the piles of laundry downstairs, a few of the men in the boarding house demanded their bathwater, too. She placed more wood in the kitchen stove and refilled the pots. Once she delivered all the bathwater, each return trip would be with a five-gallon bucket of dirty water in each hand.

There was a flat stick carved into an oar to stir the clothes once she had finished heating bathwater. Boiling the sheets was the only way to remove the stains. Her arms would ache, her neck would hurt and the thirteen steps would add up to a mile before nightfall, but at least it wasn't a hospital full of dying men. Somerset, her friend from church, worked longer hours at a hospital for less pay and still slept on a cot in the church basement. This job came with meals and room in the kitchen for a cot when the day's chores ended. Not fancy, but warm and private. She'd slept in worse places. She picked up an armful of wood from the dwindling pile and set it next to the stove.

No wonder the last maid disappeared. If I don't figure out an easier way to keep this house clean, this job's gonna own me. But I ain't for sale. Nobody owns me. Nobody's stopping me from looking for another job while I keep this one, neither. Got to take care of myself best I can. Much as I love Joe, can't be waiting on him forever. Got to get on with my life—even if it feels like it's already over.

Rachel endured her first week at Miss Hall's boarding house. Her job came with Sundays off without pay, and although Mondays came with two days' worth of work, in three more weeks she could put money in the collection plate at church. For now, however, she kept her hands beneath a shawl. She devoted the morning of her first day off from work to the church, and would spend the afternoon working as a healer. She knew Grandma was still watching over her and wanted it this way.

Somerset worked at the Cincinnati Marine Hospital and had asked Rachel to accompany her after church. The hospital was full of soldiers, and the cavernous ward resonated with the sounds of men conversing or moaning. Some of the men were playing poker and the slap of cards hitting a wooden table echoed off the dome-shaped ceiling. The rustle of bedclothes, a clink from glass tubes rattling together; with so many competing noises, it was safe for Rachel and Somerset to talk openly.

"Working for Miss Hall make a week seem like a month. The cleaning never stops."

Somerset shrugged. "Mostly dying going on here, but there might be some good come out of it—why I asked you to come today. Follow me." Somerset led her out of the ward, into the narrow alley. She pointed to a mound of blankets. "Somebody was just throwing these away."

Rachel picked a blanket off the top of the pile. "Boiling these with some walnut husks ought to cover the bloodstains—"

"Nurse!"

Somerset ignored the shout and grabbed the blanket on top of the pile. "Help me fold this so the worst is inside."

"You ain't gonna see what he needs?"

"Already know. Let's load up these blankets before somebody changes their mind about throwing them out."

"Nurse! God damn it to hell. Where the hell's a nurse?"

"Think you oughta go?" Rachel asked. "I can finish up here."

"Won't do no good." Somerset reached for another blanket. "Just another pleasure seeker."

"Huh?"

"Addicted to morphine. That's what we call 'em: pleasure seekers. Yankee doctors handing out pills like they was free candy."

Rachel folded another blanket. "Been giving out slippery elm bark and sassafras root for pain. Ain't had nobody complain." Honey and lemon juice for sore throats, clove oil and belladonna to alleviate teething pain, a contraband camp filled with crying children gradually quieted when she visited.

"Nurse!"

Somerset pretended not to hear.

"Son of a bitch! I'm hurting over here. Where the hell's a nurse?"

Rachel paused mid-fold. "That voice sound a little familiar."

"Wouldn't know about that." Somerset reached for another blanket.

"The way he swears sounds rememberable, too."

"Don't pay him no mind. That one started out mad. He ain't likely to get no better." Somerset pushed a stack of blankets under a discarded three-legged table. "Could use some help with him, though."

Helping out is what a friend does. Guess this makes us friends. Think I'm a little out of practice, though. Ain't had no friend since Joe and me was kids. When she thought of Joe, prayer naturally followed. *Lord, keep watching over him. I know he's alive. I know he's thinking about me, too.*

You and me the only ones who know he's got it in him to get free—

"I'll just peek around this corner, first." Somerset put her arm out to stop Rachel from walking into the ward. "You want to watch yourself around that white boy—and his brother. He got enough mean for an army."

Rachel glanced at her friend, saw how she clenched her teeth and set her face to mask the pain and anger. Somerset didn't get much pay, did twice the work of the white nurses, and probably wouldn't get a pension, but with the passage of the Emancipation Proclamation, this was a holy war for freedom.

Somerset straightened her posture and stepped through the doorway into the ward. Rachel stopped as soon as she saw the patient. Sickly pale skin, hair looking like it was on fire and a face full of freckles, it was the way he cussed that clinched it.

"What in the goddamn hell you looking at?"

"Bo Magruder!"

"He ain't here, yet." Sheridan, Bo's younger brother, was propped up in bed and missing a leg that still hurt. Sometimes it itched, too, he complained, but mostly it smelled bad and the doctors kept cutting on it. "Get me a white nurse, damnit." He winced and sucked in his breath with a sharp hiss. "Starting to feel poorly."

"I got something for your pain." Somerset kept the expression from her face and focused her gaze on the wall behind him. "I can ease your pain or you can keep hollering and wait some more."

"Then hurry up. But don't think I ain't gonna be watching you."

"Be outta your way soon as I can." Somerset looked toward Rachel and pointed at a wheeled cart with a set of shelves containing rows of bottles and stacks of bandages. "Bring me that bottle on the end."

Rachel didn't move. "Your brother? Bo's your brother?"

"I already said he wasn't here, bitch. You deaf or just ignorant?" Sheridan glared at Rachel. "Get your ass over there and get me my pills."

"Here." Somerset wheeled the cart next to Sheridan's bed and shook a couple of pills into her hand. "Take these and be quiet. We got work to do."

"Shut the hell up. You ain't giving me no orders." Sheridan grabbed the pills and swallowed them without water.

Like most white folk, once the women started their chores the white men ignored them. Black people became invisible in the white world when they were working.

Rachel helped Somerset change the sheets, but it felt like she was sleepwalking her way through a bad dream.

Bo Magruder's brother—God must be feeling white. Ain't no bounty hunter alive that respects the north side of the Ohio River. No such thing as a free state for a run-away slave. Once Bo finds out where I am, he's coming after me. Too much reward money for him to leave me alone. But where can I go?

A pall of smoke hung in a low cloud over the city. The soot made Rachel's chest hurt with each breath, and the air carried a heavy odor of smoke and ash. She skirted the army encampment on the banks of the Ohio River. The tents were erected on wooden floors to keep the partially reclaimed swampland from swallowing the soldiers whole, but mud churned by four thousand horses and ten thousand men clung to everything less than a foot off the ground. Mold grew on the sides of tents. The canvas leaked when it rained and sweated moisture when the sun came out. At night, man and tent froze. The ambulance ships docked at the piers formed a stark reminder of Confederate victories.

She glanced at the evening sky, and saw a smoke trail blotting out a wide swath of stars. The smell was stronger once she passed over the canal, worse than the typical coal-and-wood smoke that enveloped the city in wintertime. She held her arm up to her face and pressed her nose against her coat sleeve to keep from choking on the fumes. An oily smoke cloud obscured the path that wound between the tenements. She navigated by touch, but could see flames when she turned onto Third Street.

"Oh God! It's the church." She ran.

The front vestibule of the sanctuary was on fire. The entire roof smoldered. Thick black smoke curled from beneath the shingles, and on the alley side of the church, the paint had blackened from the heat. A fresh cloud of steam billowed from the walls with each bucketful of water but it looked like the fire was gaining. Deacon Turner sat on the ground a few feet away from the church, so close to the fire she could see the flames reflected in his glassy eyes. There was nothing left of his eyelashes but a few tiny white buds resting against his eyelids. His eyes were so bloodshot, she couldn't see any white. A few tufts of hair survived from his scraggly beard, but these were scorched and emphasized the pockmarks on the rest of his face. Ash covered what little hair remained on his head. Rachel noticed a bandana tied around his right hand.

"Some children was playing in the loft," he wiped tears away with his good hand. "Got two of 'em out, all I could carry. Couldn't get back up the stairs. Heard 'em screaming. I tried. I—just couldn't get past the flames. Them kids kept screaming. Thought they'd never stop." He closed his eyes and shuddered. "It was worse when they got quiet."

"Who were they?" she asked, thinking of Mrs. Smith's children.

"Don't know. Couldn't get no closer to see. Reached out my hand through the flames. Held it there long as I could. They never took it."

"Let's get you somewhere so I can take a look at those burns."

"No. I—need to help. This wind picks up any, whole church is gonna catch."

"Need to see 'bout those burns."

"Later. I can still use my good hand."

"At least let me make you a sling." She used her bonnet to cradle his elbow and tied the straps around the back of his neck for support. She rested his injured hand against his chest and secured his arm with a strip of cloth ripped from the hem of her coat. "There. Now at least it won't get hurt worse."

He used his good hand to help carry empty buckets back to the well. She joined the bucket line and passed water across the street from the well in the boardinghouse basement. White bystanders gathered in the street. Light from the flames turned their hate-filled faces a satanic red, flickering yellowish light gave their exposed teeth a devilish cast. They cheered when the roof over the foyer collapsed. A little white boy held his father's hand and chanted along with the crowd, "Burn! Burn! Burn!" His little sister sat on her father's shoulders so she could see above the crowd, too young to chant but not too young to learn about hate. She clapped her hands together each time a section of the roof collapsed and sent a flurry of sparks skyward. The black bystanders helped but most of them disappeared when the first white man wearing a badge arrived at the scene.

The parishioners' frantic efforts failed to save the front of the church. The entryway and the loft directly above it were reduced to a spent funeral pyre, and ashes from the children trapped upstairs intermingled with the foyer's remains. When no more flames were evident and a pool of filthy water covered the front entry and formed puddles in the street, Rachel persuaded Deacon Turner to follow her to the basement so she could tend to his burns.

"You sure it's safe to go down there?" he asked.

"Ain't got nowhere else to go." She had to take him by his good hand before he was willing to put down his bucket.

Gray stains discolored the basement walls. The ash responsible for the damage floated on top of ankle-deep water. The basement ceiling sagged, water dripped from the cracks and formed puddles on the tables and chairs. The bucket brigade re-formed to carry water out of the building. People used shovels, their hands, anything to push the water back into the buckets.

Rachel stripped a wool blanket from one of the cots and used it to push most of the water off the tables nearest the stove. A damp streak of grime remained but it would do for now. "Lay down here." She helped Deacon Turner up to the table. "All the stove wood's wet, but we got folks looking for blankets and firewood to get you warmed back up."

"Not sure if I can stand any more fire," he said, seeing her open the woodstove's door.

"Me neither, but you'll catch your death if we don't get you warm and dry. Got to do something to warm this place up and start drying it out."

A compress of diluted vinegar cooled the skin and helped with the pain. She ground lavender and set a few cotton bolls on fire. A paste made with lavender leaves mixed with cotton ash worked best for burns. She covered the poultice with honey so it would stay in place.

"Thanks," he said. "Now I need to help." He tried to get up, but only made it as far as a slouched-over sitting position.

"You need to lay back down and rest." She placed a hand on his chest. A light touch was all it took to make him change his mind. "C'mon, now," she lowered her voice to a whisper. "Rest some. I'll watch out for you. You know we each taking our turn helping the other."

She pushed another table close to the stove and cleared the surface the best she could for the next patient. In between, she heated pots of water to boiling on the stove. Long after midnight when the last injured person was as comfortable as she could make them, she bowed her head and prayed aloud so God would pay attention.

"Keep watching over Joe. Send some lightning bolts or make some thunder loud enough for him to hear, anything to let him know I ain't give up on him."

CHAPTER EIGHTEEN

Joe raised his right hand and swore an oath. He didn't know his birthday or the exact date of the birth of his son, but he would always remember the first day of March in 1864 because he wore the blue uniform of the US Colored Infantry. He gave his word to continue the fight for freedom. His shirt had an eagle on every button; his light blue pants were wool and had a dark blue stripe on the outside edges. He had new boots, clothes without any holes, and his first warm coat, but his rifle was his most prized possession. Joe was the best shot in the regiment.

"I imagine it's Old Shaky," he said. "Trues my aim right up."

He learned to read and make marks because he did without sleep to study. "The white man kept me stupid," Joe said, when his bunkmates asked him to blow out the candles if the light was keeping them awake. "Don't mean I got to stay that way."

Some of the men complained about the rations, calling the canned meat, "embalmed beef" or "salt horse." The soldiers criticized the cook for serving biscuits that had more weevils than flour and bad-mouthed his lumpy gravy made from "condemned milk."

Joe peeled the crust off his biscuits since most of the insects rose to the top during baking. "A hungry man's a fool if he complain about what he's eating." He chewed the lumps in the gravy and ignored the taste. "Best meal I ate today," he said, if it was break-fast. Lunch and dinner might pass without a compli-ment, but he never complained about having three meals a day after mostly starving as a slave.

Joe learned how to be his own man. The leader in him who once lay dormant, the quality the white man feared when he was a slave, was the inner strength that shaped him into a soldier worth promoting. Joe realized that his innate ability to fix any machine was the same sort of skill necessary to command soldiers and he developed into the kind of officer who earned the respect of his troops. Soldiers under his command followed orders because he didn't give any orders he wouldn't carry out himself. When the directive came to move out, it was Joe who led the troops toward battle.

Joe and the men under his command fought for control of roads and railroads, fought one trench at a time against a Confederate Army in place long before they marched onto the scene. The Southern Volunteer Army held the high ground on every hill the United States Colored Soldiers approached, and were dug in behind earthen works at every stream or river they had to ford. Every ditch Joe crossed on Confederate soil had Succesh dug in on the other side, the side most easily defended. The South used young boys who cried when the first shot was fired, or gray-haired men too old to march as a rear guard. When the fighting started, and while the Union soldiers fought the reserves and townspeople, the Confederate Army circled around to attack from behind.

Joe saw the smoke from their rifles before he heard the bullets flying overhead. One of the minie balls struck the man next to him and splattered his blood on Joe's shirt. The man fell, dead before his shattered head rested on the ground beside Joe. The sight unnerved him.

But I been trained to fight. Ain't nuthin else to do. Only way outta here is through. Fighting my way to you, Rachel. Don't know where you are, but I'm going through hell to get there.

The railroad bridge was one hundred yards past a shallow ditch that sloped the wrong way. The next man to peek over the embankment was shot in the jaw. "Stay low," the man next to him screamed. "We got to lay in the mud."

"Charge!" Joe was the first man out of the ditch. The men who followed him couldn't see how hard it was for him to keep his eyes open, didn't hear him whimper the first time a shell exploded close enough to throw dirt in his face. It was rock and luck that saved him from the first bullet. He stubbed his toe on the rock, stumbled, heard the minie ball whistle by his ear but kept running. One of the men behind him screamed when the bullet meant for Joe struck him in the chest. Joe aimed at a man who was pointing his rifle at him and shot first. No one was a better shot than Joe, and it saved him. He kept attacking, looking for confederate targets in his rifle sights.

When one of the townspeople missed, it saved him.

When one of the young boys screamed instead of firing his rifle, it saved him.

When one of the old men took too long to reload his rifle, it saved him. No one was faster at reloading than Joe. He fired first, and became one of the lucky ones.

Don't feel lucky, but don't make no sense feeling sorry for myself when I'm digging another man's grave.

He buried the men he had served with and watched out for the men who survived. The battle over the railroad line lasted until the rain came. The ground turned to mud, then the water drained to the low side of the field where Joe and his men used a ditch as cover. It rained through most of the night and when the morning mists cleared, the Confederates had retreated sometime during the night. Joe posted guards and set pickets, made certain the men under his command were as safe as he could make them and as well-cared-for as conditions allowed. His biggest challenge: bushwhackers, Confederate snipers who let the white Union troops march past and lay in wait for the opportunity to fire upon the men of the US Colored Troops.

"Cut down those trees over there," Joe ordered the men under his command. "Cut up them dead branches, too. Build a bonfire across these rails."

When the railroad track was as hot as the fire could make it, they cut down green trees and used the limber branches to bend the metal rails into pretzel shapes, working under Joe's order to twist the track into loops and figure eights. Once twisted, the rails were forever ruined, impossible to straighten no matter how many blacksmith blows rained down upon the metal. When the Succesh trains couldn't move supplies, the Rebel army ran out of everything it needed to keep fighting. It was a brilliant Union strategy but hugely unpopular with the loyal slave owners left behind by the Rebel army's retreat.

When the camp was set to Union soldiering standards and all the men under his command were fed, Joe made his way to where the dog robber, the soldier who cooked for the men, had set up.

"Grab a root, sir," the dog robber said. "Got carrots today. Helps make up for the embalmed beef."

In spite of the heat and his fatigue, Joe smiled, recalling his introduction to canned meat. Fresh vegetables that grew in the ground were "roots."

The dog robber wrapped the bottom of his apron around his hand and used a metal ladle to fill Joe's plate with fresh carrots and embalmed beef stew. "You just off picket, sir?"

"No. Just come from checking on it, though." Joe balanced a slab of cornbread on top of the unidentifiable chunks. "Been busy making sure camp gets set."

"Ain't hurt your appetite none, sir."

"These vittles is top rail."

"Because they Union beans, sir. Why they taste so good."

Joe narrowed eyes and cocked his head the way he did when he was figuring out how something worked. "Union beans?"

"Yes, sir. Massa told me I was free ten months ago. Yankees was getting close, so he didn't want to take no chance on getting shot on account of being Succesh. I makes my mark on a paper the way a free man do. Massa promised me one-fifth of what I grows the first year and one-third the next. I goes back to work in the fields, but when I ask for my share, he say, 'You ain't getting none. Them is last year's beans. You still a slave when they was planted,' he told me." He shook his head at the betrayal, but smiled when he looked across the field where he once slaved. "Massa been run off for good and I'd tell him good riddance if I got the chance. Yankee general using his house for headquarters now."

Joe mopped up what was left of his beans with the last hunk of johnnycake. "Good to be eating Union beans. Plan on shooting as many Union bullets as I can carry tomorrow."

"Then you'd best keep up your strength, sir. Hold out your plate..."

Later that night, Joe sewed his name on the back of his uniform shirt so his body could be identified. His men gathered around small scattered fires. They sat far enough away from the flames to avoid being Confederate targets, but close enough so the smoke chased away the mosquitoes. The men without a "housewife" waited their turn to borrow his needle. His sewing kit, or "housewife," was donated by the Civil War Women's Relief Corps. A simple cloth bag with red drawstrings, it contained needles, thread, buttons and scissors.

"First shot the hardest," a soldier who took pride in his uniform said. "Sewing my name on the back of my shirt, on account of it being likely I'm gonna die tomorrow, coming in a close second."

"Shoot or be shot, kill or be kilt make it easier to decide." Joe handed the soldier next to him the needle. He took little part in such talk. He was in command and might have to order these men to their deaths. He couldn't be their friend. It was hard to make peace with death having experienced so little of life, yet he'd heard that nearly one-third of the US Colored troops had lost their lives, with more losses sure to come. He might be next, but until that happened, he was fighting so he could be with Rachel and their child. The knowing about Rachel had never left him, although the pain she carried was unfamiliar.

In his tent, he started another letter to her. Schooling didn't come easy for him, but he never quit learning marks. Learning to read had brought his promotion. His leadership abilities came naturally. Trying to find words for the woman who meant everything to him was a struggle.

> Rachel,
>
> Dont giv up on me none I ain't give up on you. Fight my way to you all the way to where Mr. Lincoln say we can live free. All the way to Canady if I needs to.
>
> Lov, Joe

There was so much more to say, but not enough marks to let her know how much he missed her. He gently pressed a fold into the middle of the paper so the marks wouldn't smear before they dried, then cradled the letter in both hands and closed his eyes so the thoughts could go on ahead.

Been a year and a half since I seen you and it feels like a lifetime. Ain't never forgot you, Rachel. Ain't never stopped loving you, neither. In that way we got of knowing 'bout each other, I know you ain't forgot me.

He printed her name and "Washington, D.C." on the envelope. That's where Mr. Lincoln lived and he promised they could be free.

Rachel hung her good dress on a peg next to the stove. She straightened the collar and ran her fingers down the pleats so the material wouldn't wrinkle. A peculiar smell of smoke and ash emanated from the simple blue cloth. The church building was ruined but the congregation remained strong. She had spent the night in the church basement tending to the people injured in the fire and the talk was about rebuilding. With a promise to return, she had hurried back to her job. She had nowhere else to go.

She added wood to the firebox and filled the cast iron pots on top of the stove with water. Miss Antoinette took a bath every morning. Rachel carried a five-gallon bucket in each hand, almost 100 pounds of hot water. Mostly from habit, she counted the 13 steps from the stove to the backdoor of the boardinghouse, and then trudged up two flights of stairs and walked to the end of a long hallway. The locks on Miss Antoinette's door clicked open before Rachel raised her hand to knock.

"You're late," Miss Antoinette pointed toward the dressing table. "Put down the water and read that poster."

"Poster?"

"Don't act stupid with me. I know you can read." The honey in her voice couldn't cover the poison in her words. "Aloud," she added, when Rachel picked up the copy.

A yellowed piece of paper rested beneath the mirror on the dressing table. The ink was faded from being in the sun. There was a hole in the top with a rust stain from the nail that once held it in place, but the printing was legible, the description unmistakable.

"Reward offered, for information leading to the capture of a young slave woman. Answers to the name of Rachel." The reward for her return was enough money to make a priest give up his vows.

"Go on," Miss Antoinette snapped. "Keep reading."

"Don't recognize the rest of these words," she lied. *Recognize that description, though. Every time I make the mistake of looking in a mirror.*

"That's you it's asking about."

"No, ma'am. Just some poor woman bearing a little resemblance to me."

"Don't lie to me. I saw this and recognized you before I finished the first sentence."

"Like I said before. Strange coincidence. I'll just pour out this water and get back to cleaning."

"Read down to that part that mentions a baby."

Rachel felt her palms sweating and looked down: the sweat was making the bloodstains on her hands glow with the peculiar look she recognized from her nightmares. She clenched her teeth against the shakes. "Wouldn't know about that, ma'am. Like I said, that ain't me—just a powerful coincidence."

"Perhaps."

Rachel looked into Miss Antoinette's green eyes. They were slave-owner eyes.

She's up to no good. I see it in those green eyes she got from sleeping with the Devil. See it in the way she's caressing the seven deadly sins engraved on her locket.

"I think I'll find out who paid for this notice."

CHAPTER NINETEEN

The May rains of 1864 brought torrential June showers, but a porch covered the steps leading away from the new church building. Rachel draped a scarf over her head and tied it. She let her umbrella rest against her shoulder. The war showed no sign of ending and bad weather only made it worse. She'd heard of thirteen thousand casualties at Cold Harbor, five thousand of them in the first hour of fighting. Wounded soldiers came by ship, train and horse-drawn ambulance to the hospitals and many of them were colored troops. The rain let up a moment. A rainbow appeared and reminded her of the colorful sash Grandma always wore.

Keep watching over Joe, Grandma. I feel your gaze when I look up at the North Star. I know you're with me during every Promise Moon. Hear your voice in the way the wind rustles the leaves, or how it sways the little branches at the tops of trees. Joe's alive, I know it because you let me feel it. As long as you keep giving me hope, I know you're watching over him, too.

Rachel followed the back alleys and hidden paths of Smoketown—Cincinnati's colored district and unseen backyard. Shacks and slave quarters sat at the back of the grand properties, hidden among narrow alleys and dead-end streets. She sidestepped piles of trash and avoided the rats scurrying underfoot. The few people she passed shared averted gazes, an unspoken but understood etiquette among those with conditional freedom.

That's what I got. She hung her good dress on a peg next to the stove. *Until this war ends, I got a second-class freedom. Never feel it so strong as when I come back to start another week of work.*

She boiled bathwater and carried it through the back door. Miss Antoinette met her in the kitchen. "Follow me," she said, "and keep your mouth shut."

She led Rachel to the top of the stairs, but paused in the hallway while a drunken boarder staggered down the hall. He lost his balance, fell against the wall with a heavy thump, caromed off the opposite wall, then regained his footing and tromped down the stairway.

Miss Antoinette eased the door ajar when the hallway was empty—

"Get me a doctor!" A man yelled as soon as the door started moving. "You out there. You hear me? Call a Goddamn doctor!"

Miss Antoinette peered inside the room, and then turned to Rachel. "Ignore him. You're here to clean up. Not a word of this to anybody." She locked the door after they entered the room and slipped the key into a pocket sewn on the inside of her dress.

Dark furniture hewn from solid wood looked heavy enough for the house to have been built around it. An armoire on the opposite wall displayed a diverse collection of leather and whips. Strong perfume couldn't hide the sourness of stale sweat soaked into the leather. The pungent odor of an unwashed body permeated the room. The view through the bedroom window was of the military encampment; the view of the man lying on the floor next to the bed, trouble.

Freckles splattered across the man's forehead matched his flushed cheeks. A knife scar gave him a squinty eye and bisected the middle of his lower lip, but his crooked nose leaned toward the left side of his face. "What the hell?"

Rachel froze. *Bo Magruder! How'd he find me?*

"Don't just stand there," Miss Antoinette said to Rachel. "Clean this mess up." She held her right hand at shoulder height. "Five." She flexed her fingers twice so there was no mistake. "You have five minutes."

"What the hell? What are you—" A spasm doubled Bo over. He nearly choked on the bile.

With the deliberate maneuver of a jackal as it eased toward a fresh kill, Miss Antoinette moved to where Bo lay on the floor. She rested a hip on the edge of the bed and leaned over him. "Shall we talk about hijacked medical supplies or the counterfeit greenbacks you've been passing?"

Beads of sweat formed along his receding hairline. He swayed and half-rolled to a sitting position on the floor. It reminded Rachel of how the round-hulled morgue ships rocked back and forth where they tied up along the river.

"You!" He pointed toward Rachel. "You ain't getting away this time. Ain't taking no chances—"

"How dare you ignore me." Miss Antoinette put her hands on her hips. "Pay attention when I'm talking to you."

"Shut up you ignorant bitch. There's a rewar—"

"Don't interrupt me!"

"She," Bo pointed toward Rachel, but a spasm interrupted. He crawled away from the bed and retched in the direction of a chamber pot.

Miss Antoinette lifted her fancy shoe off the floor and pointed its toe toward the vomit next to the bed. "Wipe this up," she ordered.

Rachel pulled a rag from her apron pocket. There wasn't enough rag for the mess, and the water basin rested on the stand beside Bo.

God help me. Gonna have to clean this up so she'll unlock the door.

"Got you." Bo grasped her arm.

"Let go of her." Miss Antoinette grabbed Bo's wrist. His fingers were slippery with vomit and his hand slid off Rachel's arm when Miss Antoinette pulled on his wrist.

Lord, help me. Caught in the middle means losing on both ends. Rachel prayed the heartfelt prayers of the desperate, but maybe God was taking a nap. Maybe He didn't hear or was too busy to help.

"Damnit, listen up. That bitch is—"

Miss Antoinette interrupted. "I told you to shut up."

"But—" A wave of nausea snapped Bo's mouth shut. He gagged and put a hand over his mouth.

Rachel glanced at the mirror and saw Miss Antoinette's heartless green eyes staring at her. She averted her gaze to the washbasin and grabbed the bar of soap next to it. The soap nearly slid from her fingers. The corners were rounded from use and greasy: hog fat and wood ash cooked down to a yellowish, waxy lump. When she started to wring out the rag, the blood of her nightmares began to drip from her fingertips. The bright red drops were as real as her memory could make them, as real as the nightmares she had of that awful day when her baby's blood dripped from her hands. It would take more than soap to become clean. She might as well try to scrub the color from her skin until it bled, like she had as a little girl, trying to be white. Grandma understood, she had held her and soothed her wounds with fatback and bacon grease. But Grandma was dead now. Everyone she loved was gone. Mama was sold downriver. She'd left her husband behind. Her child ... *Oh God.*

She scrubbed her hands until they were lost beneath the soap bubbles, until the water turned the bright red of the blood Samuel coughed up from his lungs.

"What are you doing?" Miss Antoinette asked.

"Nuthin'."

"You wash your hands harder than anyone has a need to."

"Just making double sure, ma'am."

"Hmm." Miss Antoinette stared with the intense concentration of a hungry carnivore as it stalks its prey. "Don't lie to me."

"Uh ..." Rachel glanced at Bo. His face was redder than she'd ever seen. He still had his hand over his mouth but it wouldn't stay there forever.

Best clean up this mess and get out of here. Soon as Bo stops gagging, he's gonna start talking. Soon as Miss Antoinette hears about the reward for my capture, I ain't never getting away from this house.

She turned her back toward both of them and kneeled to wipe vomit from the floor. She closed her eyes so she wouldn't have to look at the bloodstains on her wet hands. Samuel's blood made her fingers take on a strange, luminous glow. She saw the ghostly trace of his blood no matter where she looked or how hard she closed her eyes.

"I asked you a question."

"Yes, ma'am." She scrubbed at the vomit. The rag needed to be rinsed. *God help me. Where you at Grandma?*

"You hear me? Why do you wash your hands so hard?"

"Sorry to be slow, ma'am. I'll get this mess cleaned right up." She closed her eyes and plunged the rag into the water, rinsing it first before scrubbing it clean with soap. She twisted the rag to wring the excess water out and opened her eyes to place the soap back in the dish. Instead, she saw those pale green eyes with their hooded lids. She looked away and saw Bo gasping for breath.

Miss Antoinette watched Rachel in the mirror. She spread her lips in a predator's smile and revealed incisors yellowed by tobacco smoke. If a snake possessed teeth, it would bare such a smile while it eyed its prey. Bottomless black dots formed the centers of her eyes, and they seemed to see right through her. Rachel glanced from her to Bo. His face held a similar predatory look.

Unable to avoid one without looking at the other, she stared at the floor. She couldn't look up without seeing those eerie green eyes; she couldn't look down without being haunted by the nightmare of blood on her hands. She couldn't put her hands back into the water because it was already stained with her baby's blood. She closed her eyes and fumbled for the soap. *Hog fat.* Her bloody fingers recoiled from the slippery texture. Nothing smelled worse than butchering hogs. Burning the hair off carcasses or emptying intestines for sausage casings, everything about hogs was nasty, and the vilest thing of all was rendering the fat and leftover mess into soap.

You have to do this. Only way outta this trouble is moving through it. Got to make it to the other side of that door. She drew in a searing breath. In one determined motion, she grabbed the soap and thrust her hands into the water, but once she started to scrub, she couldn't stop.

"Slave," Bo said. He spit the taste of vomit from his mouth and pointed a damning finger toward Rachel. "She's a runaway slave."

Rachel edged close to the fireplace and lunged for the poker. The handle burned her palm but she held on to it. "I'm leaving," she brandished the poker as a club, "and you ain't stopping me."

Miss Antoinette reached into her pocket. "Only holds one bullet," she aimed a pearl-handled derringer at Rachel's stomach, "but it's enough. Already killed one man with it. Took him a long time to die."

She's too far away for me to hit. Maybe if I throw this poker I can jump out of the way before she fires that gun.

"Ask her about the baby," Bo said.

Rachel looked at her hands. The sweat on her palms made Samuel's bloodstains glow with the peculiar look she recognized from her nightmares. She clenched her teeth against the shakes that threatened to make her legs too weak to stand.

"There's a reward," Bo added.

"Tell me about this baby." Miss Antoinette caressed the seven deadly sins engraved on her locket. "The one you ran away with."

"Don't know nothing 'bout that."

"You're lying." Miss Antoinette rested her fingertips against "wrath" and "envy." "Know how I can tell? You're holding your hands behind your back."

As most slave children did, Rachel learned how to cry without making a sound. When that no longer worked, she crossed her arms on the top of the dresser and rested her head on the inside of her forearms to muffle the sobs. The room at the end of the hall was little more than a bed and a dressing table, no different from a furnished prison cell except the carpet and thick velour drapes were of high quality. Black paint covered the windowpanes and the sash was nailed shut to prevent escape. The bed's four mahogany posts were taller than she was and as thick as one of Joe's legs. Leaves and vines were carved into the headboard, mosquito netting hung from the tester, but instead of looking practical, the effect was of the sort of diaphanous veil preferred by women of ill repute. The door locked on the outside, and only Bo and Miss Antoinette had the key.

She hadn't seen either of them for three days now. The water pitcher was empty and the privy was full. The hunger pains went away on the second day. On this, the third day, she was ready to die.

Better dying here than the slow death down south. If Grandma wanted me to survive, she would've helped me by now.

The mosquito netting swayed in an impossible breeze. She blinked her eyes to clear away half-formed tears and waited for the door to swing open. It didn't. She turned toward the window but it was still nailed shut. The netting gently swayed to a stop and the imprint of footsteps appeared on the carpet. Its fine Turkish weave held a shallow indentation in the shape of a heel and five toes. Before she could form a thought, the shallow impression disappeared as another footprint appeared, as though slowly pressed into the carpet. Her shoulder began to feel warm when the last footprint faded.

The light changed. The flame from the single gas-light on the wall was the same, but the room dimmed. An irregular shadow moved across the floor and crept up the wall on the far side of the lantern. Something brushed against her. Cloth of some sort, maybe a quilt, and it smelled faintly of pipe tobacco.

Light shining through the lantern's ornate base separated the shadow into ten distinct lines of unequal length. She shook her head, certain she was imagining this, until the lines merged to form a ten-pointed crown. *Satan's Gold Crown,* she thought, and put her hands behind her back in surrender. *Devil's come to burn what's left of my soul.* She ducked her head in shame and waited to be punished for killing her baby.

It got cold instead. Not frigid like the waters Samuel drowned in, but the cooling sort of breeze welcome in summer. And it smelled like the springhouse when there was mint growing nearby.

Too much pain for this to be a dream. Either I'm goin' crazy, or Grandma's crossing over from the other side and wants me to follow. Either way: go crazy and I won't care; die today and my suffering ends.

Grandma's voice came with the wind brushing a tree branch against the window. She whispered with the leaves rustling in the breeze. *I'm still here, praying you get free. But the only way you getting free is by surviving. Ain't your time to die, child. You'll have to trust me. I didn't raise no quitter. You got to hang on to life...*

Clattering wooden wheels on cobblestones announced the coming dawn as a pushcart vendor rolled by. It was Sunday, a day of rest for some, but merely another day in hell for Rachel. With no sharp objects in her room, there was nothing that could be used as a weapon or tool. The only metal in her room was the gaslight, but it was firmly anchored in the wall and encased in a metal sconce that wouldn't break no matter how often she'd tried. When all ten of her fingernails were broken, she used her teeth to weaken the wood frame that held the door hinges. She stepped back, listened. There'd been no outside noises during her work, no cry of alarm—yet.

Done about the best I can do with what little I got. I'm a sinner with no hope of salvation, but this troubled house is finally asleep. Might be my only chance to run.

It took three kicks to knock the door into the hallway. She stepped through the doorway and dragged the chair from her room. She waited.

Bo Magruder's heavy boots pounded on the stairs as he took them two at a time. There was a brief pause in his cadence as he reached the first landing. She waited for three more tromps, then held the chair so the legs pointed away from her and lunged down the stairs. The collision knocked both of them from their feet, but she used the chair and Bo to break her fall at the bottom of the stairs. The force of her momentum caused him to land halfway under a heavy side table. Recovering first, she scrambled to her feet and ran toward the back door.

"Son of a bitch," he yelled, kicked the chair away and rolled onto his hands and knees to get off the floor. "Shit!" he shouted when he bumped his head against the table's underside.

He reached for an empty whiskey bottle rolling on the floor beside him, wrapped his fingers around the neck and pounded the lower half of the bottle against a chair until the glass broke into a jagged edge. He waved the bottle and moved between the back door and the stairwell.

She knocked over a table so he couldn't reach her and grabbed a chair to use as a club. He shoved the table so it rolled toward her. She pushed it aside with one hand, but it was all the time he needed to get close enough to grab one of the chair legs before she could swing it. He tried to yank the chair out of her hands and she refused to let go, but he moved closer and pivoted on his hip. He twisted the chair until she lost her balance.

He stepped aside and grabbed a handful of her hair, then pulled her head backward until her neck felt it would snap. When she tried to kick him in the shins, he reached around with his other hand and slapped her face. He hit her again, this time with the heel of his hand against her nose. Tears blurred her eyes. He slapped her again and her right cheek burned with the imprint of his fingers.

"Not in the face!" Miss Antoinette was at the top of the stairs. "Bring her upstairs before someone sees you."

Bo looked up, startled by her sudden appearance.

Rachel took advantage of the interruption. She grabbed his hand, dug her fingernails into both sides of his wrist and bit his forearm. He let go of her hair. She stomped on the arch of his foot and slid out of his grasp, ran across the room, yanked open the door and ran toward the trash heap. She grabbed an up-turned bucket and scooped up some trash. She flung the bucket at Bo, then turned and ran the other way.

He limped outside and slipped on the eggshells scattered in the alley. When he started to push himself up, his hands slipped on the still-runny egg whites. "Shit!"

She ran, moving toward the west side of the contraband camp where the color of her skin might save her. Bo would stick out like a snowflake in a coal mine if he was stupid enough to follow her into the camp. She kept the canal and most of the shacks between them. There was a community garden where rows of corn offered enough cover to hide behind, yet she could peer between the stalks and see if he was still nearby. She let her top eye guide her and turned into the soft breeze. The wind carried the sound of a city in slumber: the faint ring of church bells in the distance; the lonely whisper of a barge as it floated past on the canal. Everything else was silent. She held a handkerchief to her nose to ward off the stench of raw sewage and crossed the canal seven blocks from where Bo last saw her. She approached the church from the alley side and knocked three times: twice on the door and once on the wall.

No "hello" or "who's there?" came from behind the door, only silence. She could sense rather than hear the deliberate tread of muffled footsteps approach the door. The heavy silence of fear engulfed her.

"Rachel! Almost didn't let you in." Somerset waved her inside and closed the door as soon as she stepped over the threshold.

CHAPTER TWENTY

Rachel pulled on a pair of men's pants. The legs were too long and the colors didn't match. She used a piece of cord to keep the coarse woolen pants from sliding off her hips, rolled the extra material into cuffs and pinned the fabric in place. The shirt she pulled over her head was several sizes too large and stained a strange shade of blue. She stuffed a rag into the crown of a floppy straw hat so it wouldn't hang down past her nose.

"Won't nobody recognize you in Army blanket clothes." Deacon Turner handed her a tree branch carved into a crude cane. "Limp a little. Won't nobody think you're running if you moving slow."

Somerset wore Rachel's dress and hat. The women from the sewing circle gathered in the basement.

Someone pounded on the front door. "Open up, God damn it to hell! I know that bitch is in there."

"Sounds like Bo Magruder." Rachel said.

"Sounds like he's out on the street," Somerset said. "We'll go out the front door and give him the wrong people to chase." She hugged Rachel, and then walked upstairs to the sanctuary. The women in the sewing circle followed.

The strange kind of quiet that sneaks up on folks when there's trouble settled in. Deacon Turner closed his eyes to pray. Rachel felt her palms start sweating. She closed her eyes so she wouldn't have to look at the bloodstains.

A man shouted. The profanity belonged to Bo Magruder, but the thick walls of the church muffled the voices. It sounded like a mob.

Beneath the tumult, two faint, fast taps on the back door, followed by a long pause, then one short tap on the side of the building let Deacon Turner know it was safe to come outside. Mrs. Smith's little girl, the quiet one, pointed toward the north.

"They went that way?" he asked.

She nodded.

"Then let's go the other," he held one finger to his lips and motioned for Rachel to step outside. "Means we following the Whitewater Canal Tunnel." He handed her the cane and casually walked away from the church. Rachel limped alongside him.

"Didn't know what we'd need," he admitted, "so I brought a little of everything." A canvas tarp strained to cover the mountain of supplies in the back of his wagon.

"Where we headed?"

"South—last place Bo Magruder gonna look."

"What?" She forgot to limp.

"Colored troops is finally getting the chance to fight. Figure they gonna need something and a little bit of everything. Got medical supplies, cigars, candy, shoelaces, chewing tobacco, playing cards, lye soap and everything else I could find."

"But south?" She leaned on her cane. "Don't seem all that long ago we was coming the other way."

"Who else gonna look out for the colored troops? If they fighting, they sure to need healing—probably more than supplies."

"Ain't arguing the right of it, just can't help being scared. Different kind of scared, maybe. Different kind of worry, too."

"How's that?"

"More scared for Joe than myself. There's a knowing part of me that's sure he alive."

"Don't want to add to your troubles, but how you so sure?"

"Don't exactly know." She struggled to put her feelings into words. "Always had a special knowing about each other. It ain't never gone away."

If there's a God, let Him hear my prayers for Joe. If there's a God, the next time I run, it'll be with Joe by my side.

"How you so sure he's fighting?"

"The scared part of always knowing—top eye, maybe. No other way to explain it."

"If that what your top eye telling you, makes sense to listen. Ain't steered us wrong yet. What's it say about where we headed?"

"Gonna be bad. Don't need no second sight to see that far ahead."

Rachel placed her clothing for the next day, a gray calico dress and white apron, under her blanket so it would stay dry, then set some coffee grounds to a steady smolder. The smoke helped cover the stench and keep the mosquitoes away. At each battleground, contraband soldiers were kept separate from the white army but less than a mile from the battlefield. In this case, that meant nearest the swamp and downwind of the trash mound. She shared a hut with the other battlefield nurses who treated the survivors and helped bury the dead. There were plenty of both outside Petersburg, Virginia; wounded and dying filled every cot in the field hospital. The siege was in its second month, and July 1864 was unseasonably hot, with little respite from hundred-degree days featuring hundred-percent humidity. When added to the tedious boredom between battles and substandard food, morale was at its lowest since she arrived.

Doctors, nurses and injured men received the same rations as soldiers: black beans, embalmed beef and coffee. When there was nothing else to eat, the men broke up weevil-infested hardtack and put it in their muckets: cups too big to be mugs and too small to be buckets. Boiling water poured over the pieces allowed the weevils to rise to the top where they could be skimmed off and the remainder "eaten on faith." She ate what the men ate and cared for the wounded, sick and dying.

She possessed the hands of a healer. The blood-stains were mostly those of the wounded men she treated. The strange, gory luminescence of Samuel's blood that only she could see surfaced sometimes, but there was little time for personal troubles. In the aftermath of battle, the wounds were horrific and death was welcomed by many, but the ones who could be saved owed their lives to the men and women who worked in the battlefield hospitals.

Most of the fighting was on Confederate soil. Despite her dreams of the North, Rachel worked in the contraband camps and battlefields of the South.

She wouldn't head back north until her top eye told her that's where Joe was.

Malaria, typhoid, dysentery, measles, mumps, chickenpox, gangrene and sepsis took more lives than bullets. She used goose grease and sorghum mixed with turpentine and brown sugar to treat the croup. Cockleburr and blackberry root cured diarrhea. Tea brewed from cotton plant roots helped with breathing trouble. When she wasn't doctoring soldiers, she held classes, teaching the Contraband soldiers to read. Each class began with questions about Joe. That night, she held up a drawing of Joe she had commissioned with money from her first nursing paycheck.

"His name is Joe. Have you seen him?" She gave the men time to remember, time to stare at the drawing so they would recognize his face. "Heard anything? Anything at all? Please let me know. Promise me you'll look for him."

Class began after the men studied Joe's portrait and promised to let her know if they saw him. No one opened a book until she was certain his image was familiar to all of the men present. As she did each night, she read aloud from Ephesians to begin the class. The men never seemed to tire of this scripture, perhaps because they listened to it abused and misquoted so often in the white man's church:

> You shall not hand over to his master
> a slave who has taken refuge from him

> with you. Let him live with you wherever
> he chooses, in any one of your commu-
> nities that pleases him. Do not molest
> him.

"Read us that other one," one of the men asked. He was a regular student.

"Let me read that next part, Miss Rachel." This man was one of her best students and proud of his ability to "recite letters."

"My turn," the man who was her regular student said.

"You read it last time." This man kept his uniform immaculate.

"We'll take turns," she said. "I'll finish these verses and you can start on the next ones."

> And master, treat your slaves in the same
> way. Do not threaten them, since you
> know that He who is both their Master
> and yours is in heaven, and there is no
> favoritism with him.

"Huh, no favoritism," a recent arrival said. "Why Massa never pay no mind to that part?"

"Ain't never heard that read in no white man's church." This man helped bury the dead.

"Overseer skipping right on over, 'Do not threaten.' Move directly to hitting." This man was assigned a hut near the trash mound. His clothes gave off an odor that took some getting used to.

Each man took turns reading from Rachel's bible, the only book she owned. Class lasted as long as the men were willing to struggle through the words. When her last student left, she stared at the drawing and wondered where Joe was. The connection they shared meant he was still alive. She prayed it was so, for no god could be that cruel. She carefully wrapped Joe's portrait in a linen bandage and returned it to her trunk, in the special pocket sewn into the liner where it would be protected. She knelt to pray but there was nothing that hadn't already been said.

Lord, guess I'm all prayed out. Afraid my guardian angel is all tired out, too. Afraid to pray any more for Joe in case it don't come true.

At nightfall, her work wasn't done. She searched the battlefield for men who refused to die. Unconscious instead of dead, in shock or too weak to call out for help, some men got left behind. Soldiers from both sides recognized her lantern as it moved about the battlefield and held their fire. Usually. She pinned a small red ribbon to her dress and patted it whenever the fear of being shot made it too hard to keep looking.

No survivors tonight. Too hot to sleep. She moved a cot outside and unfolded it. Closed her eyes but sleep wouldn't come. It was not the threat of nightmares that kept her awake but the promise of battle and the inevitable carnage that followed, death on a massive scale: slaughter. Neither side would win this battle, but one side would lose more. *Who's gonna be missing from the next class?*

The frogs and crickets were the last to be silent. All that was left was the ever-present buzz of flying insects and the occasional hoot from an owl. She lay awake until the haunting cry of a mourning dove warned of the coming day. The camp cook's persistent cough followed, so she mixed a tincture of sage and honey to help with his chronic sore throat. Lobelia tea controlled his coughing fits during the daytime, but there was nothing she could do about the evening mists, persistent dampness and poor living conditions.

She crouched close to the glow from the banked embers of the cooking fire. Flames sprouted from the kindling as the cook breathed new life into the coals. Smoke drifted across the camp and the smell of freshly brewed coffee edged aside the rank odor of decomposing trash. This was farm country, and the clank of cast iron pots meant the men would at least have a hearty breakfast before today's battle. For some it would be their last meal.

Please God. Don't let it be Joe.

CHAPTER TWENTY-ONE

Joe inspected the men under his command. His platoon was ready, and discipline built through routine and tradition has its place in warfare. His men passed morning inspection, and through pride came courage. They were ready to fight.

Cinque's report the night before had been troubling. It was July 30, 1864, and Joe knew this might be the last battle for many of the men under his command. After weeks spent tunneling beneath the Confederate trenches outside Petersburg, Virginia, Union troops were about to explode eight thousand pounds of black powder beneath the Rebel army's 18th and 22nd South Carolina Regiments.

"Prepare to move out," Joe ordered. He didn't need to shout. If it was shooting practice or battle, he led by example and treated everyone in his command with dignity and respect.

He marched beside his men, led them toward the enemy and into firing range, less than a ten-minute march from their camp. "We fighting at the Mine."

Their faces remained resolute.

"Fear coming," he cautioned them. "Can feel it. Can't do nothing about it except keep on with the firing."

They were in place when the expected explosion ripped through Pegram's Salient, a forward Confederate position jutting into land the Union considered its own. The massive crater created by the explosion forced a break in Confederate lines. Frightened Rebel soldiers forgot to remove the ramrods from their rifles and sent the metal rods flying like spears. Too much black powder in the pan and the explosion could singe a man's eyebrows off his face; too little powder and nothing happened. Prepackaged cartridges took some of the surprise out of each shot, though, and a well-trained soldier could fire five rounds a minute. Joe and his men bit off the paper twists of their cartridges and spit them toward the enemy before they fired. No ramrods came flying from their ranks.

By the time their fifth line fired, the first line had reloaded. There were times when one line got off two shots in the same minute. Minie balls whined as they tumbled past them in a near-miss. These conical lead bullets deformed upon impact, shattering bones and leaving gaping wounds upon exit. A man hit by a minie ball became an amputee or a fatality. A near-miss by a cannonball knocked several men to the ground. Those who weren't concussed scrambled to their feet, reloaded their rifles and kept on with the firing.

"I'm shot!" a soldier wailed. "Help me, Joe, I'm shot!"

Joe turned his head to see the soldier shrug off his jacket and rip the buttons from his shirt in his haste to examine the wound. The man next to him bent over and vomited at the sight of his buddy's intestines unwinding outside his body.

This was one of Joe's bravest soldiers, a man wounded in their first battle who had to be ordered to leave the fighting to get medical help. He crawled to the wounded man's side but there was nothing he could do for him. Slow death from complications was the only prognosis for a man shot in the stomach—for a wound this bad, it might take less than an hour for this man to die. No lie, no matter how convincing, would change the sad truth of his imminent death.

The soldier knew it too. He turned on his side and wept like a child, coughed up blood and gurgled with each pitiful attempt to breathe. A barrage of gunfire swept overhead, but the next volley was on target.

Bullets ended the wounded soldier's pain. Joe dove for cover behind the corpse and stayed close to the dirt, knowing a bullet in the forehead awaited him if he dared look up. He stayed as close to the ground as he could and reloaded his rifle by touch.

⇥ ⇤

Rachel started out on the next-to-last day of July 1864 serving in the field as a vivandier, a water carrier. The fighting began at sunrise, but she had been carrying water since dawn. Neither side fired at vivandiers, but stray bullets didn't discriminate at the Mine near Petersburg, Virginia.

Seen the elephant. The words finally made sense to Rachel when a minie ball whistled past, stopping her midstride. *Don't know who Mr. Pegram is. Ain't sure what a salient is, either, but there ain't no being scared as bad as the kind of scared like getting fired at.* It was a stray thought, but the words must have come from somewhere. *Wonder if Joe's thinking the same thing?*

When the freshwater pond turned pink with the blood of wounded and dying men who crawled there, she stopped carrying water and turned her attention to the injured.

With each return trip to the front, fewer men remained to fight and more waited on transport to the field hospital. If a man failed to time his yells between the roar from gunfire, he might lie in the same place all day. Flies settled on the dead and preyed on the weakest. The awful drone from their wings grew louder with each ambulance delivery.

Don't let it be Joe, she prayed each time an ambulance returned from the front. *Please God, don't let it be Joe. As much as I miss him, don't let me find him here.*

One of the men from her reading league, the man whose uniform smelled of garbage, grabbed the hem of her dress. "Hurt bad, Miss Rachel. Couldn't feel nothing at first. Now it hurts terrible."

She eased her hand under his neck and raised his head so he could take a sip of water, put an opium pill on his tongue and held the glass to his lips so the next swallow would take away the pain. His moans quieted. There was no need to "bite on a bullet" in this camp. Morphine was plentiful and prescribed for everything from coughs and diarrhea to removing the ungodly pain of imminent death. She moved to the next man.

The line of wounded men got longer and doubled back, then began to spread in a circle until there was no more available space. The ambulance wagons ran nonstop, the shady areas reserved for the dying filled quickly and new arrivals sweltered beneath a summer sun. The barometer of how a battle was going gave its most accurate reading with the number of wounded men delivered by ambulance. When there were more wounded than the ambulances could carry, it meant retreat was possible. If that happened, they would have to abandon the field hospital.

A line of men stood, leaned or sat outside the surgeon's tent. She stepped over the wounded when there was no room to walk around them. The stronger ones reached for her as she passed.

"Miss Rachel," the man from her reading league called. "Over here."

She went to him and asked, "How you feeling? Need something for the pain?"

"Don't feel nothing." He blinked several times, unable to focus eyes dilated by opium. "How bad is it?"

"Seen worse," she replied, and kept her voice steady. The cliché sounded hollow in her own ears, but he relaxed some at hearing them. God would forgive her this lie. "Rest up." Another euphemism, but more humane than telling him it wouldn't take long to die. Union drugs might take away his pain, but a Confederate minie ball was taking away his young life.

"Starting to feel cold, ma'am."

She took the jacket off a dead man and used it as a blanket. Neither man noticed. When the soldier's eyes closed for the last time, she returned to the surgeon's tent to see a group of newly arrived soldiers.

"Lose that leg but keep your life," she reassured a man in line for the surgeon's table. If he heard her, he gave no indication, for he wore the peculiar blank look of someone who has seen the elephant and met the demons of war.

❧

The sun reached midmorning and moved overhead. Joe's dark wool uniform heated up, dried sweat from the last battle mixing with sticky blood from the gut-shot corpse. He swallowed to force bile back down his throat. When that didn't work, he spat the taste of fear from his mouth. At a break in the gunfire, he motioned for his platoon to crawl forward and join him. "Reload," he ordered. "Fear coming, Succesh is right behi—"

The concussive blast from a Confederate cannon pounded his chest before he heard the shells shriek overhead. One explosion threw dirt on him and put the sound of church bells in his ears. He shook his head to clear the ringing and felt for blood. In one battle, he'd seen a cannonball "disappear" a man, leaving nothing to bury but his shoes. Canisters were worse: twelve or so badly formed metal balls mixed with spikes and scrap iron, encased in a canister and shot from a cannon. When the canister exploded upon impact, there was a big hole where a man used to be.

A flaming cannonball ripped through the lines and hit the soldier to Joe's left. The man's shoulder blade flew from his body, transformed into deadly shrapnel, and decapitated the soldier directly behind him. The cannonball bounced over the next line of men and cut a zigzag swath through the soldiers at the rear. Small fires marked each bounce and a tree caught fire where it came to rest.

Over the screams and gunfire came a single word: "Charge!"

Hearing this, Joe risked a peek over the corpse. An overzealous Confederate officer, assuming the US Colored Troops would run, commanded his men to advance. The first bullet through his chest alerted him to his mistake. Three more shots snuffed out his life before he fully realized the folly of his order.

"Charge!" Joe yelled in return, leaping up and over the corpse. "Time to stop hiding and start fighting!"

"Remember Fort Pillow," his platoon screamed in return. Confederate Major General Nathan Bedford Forest was rumored to have stood by while his troops killed captured US Colored Troops rather than take them prisoner. The Colored Troops adopted this battle cry after they heard of the atrocity.

Smoke from the far ridge drifted down into the valley. Dust churned up by hooves and boots met the haze until Joe couldn't see the flag up ahead. His first hint that he was running in the right direction came when the sound of rifle fire grew louder.

The Rebels waited until the Colored Troops were close, then fired canisters full of horseshoes and anchor chain. The shrapnel immediately killed an entire row of soldiers and sprayed those behind them with blood. Joe hit the ground and kept his head down as another round of metal shards flew overhead.

The Succesh charged and pushed them back, but the US Colored Troops fought an orderly retreat to the base of a nearby ridge and held their new position. Joe gathered the soldiers under his command and was preparing them for another charge as soon as reinforcements arrived, but the first men to penetrate the dust and smoke wore the wrong color uniform. *We're trapped!* He realized. *Got Succesh on all sides.* "This way," he yelled. "We got to fight our way through before they get set."

He led them partway down the ridgeline. Smoke from last night's campfires mixed with the haze from ten thousand rifles and one hundred cannons. The dust from twenty thousand pairs of feet made it impossible to see more than a few yards in either direction.

Which way do I turn? Right or left, uphill or down? Union Army headed this way, last I saw—

A barrage from the cannon on the opposite ridge exploded nearby. The shockwave knocked him to the ground. He put his hands over his ears but it didn't stop the buzzing of a hive-full of bees circling his head. He heard what he thought was gunfire and closed his eyes to listen as Rachel taught him, but that didn't help. Gunfire this loud might be from .557 caliber

British Enfield rifles the Confederates smuggled in from England, or the Union-manufactured .58 caliber Springfield musket. He couldn't tell the difference, and not knowing the difference might end his life before he got close enough to find out.

Where you at, Rachel? Which way do I go? Need your top eye to guide me.

Rachel looked up when the shadow from a spy balloon passed overhead. It might have been ten minutes, it might have been an hour since the last time she'd done anything but tend to wounded. The pilot was smoking a pipe. The semisweet smell of pipe tobacco lingered in his passing, and it was the same kind of tobacco as Grandma used to smoke. The same gentle breeze responsible for propelling the balloon overhead tugged the tattered end of a gauze bandage from her hand. She reached for the loose end and spied a four-leaf clover. No one was better than Grandma at finding a lucky leaf in a field of common plants.

Watch over Joe for me, Grandma. I'll keep sending him my top eye but you're the only one who can cross on over from the other side. Help him, Grandma, same as you been helping me.

She finished wrapping the gauze bandage around the wounded soldier and plucked the four-leaf clover from among its unremarkable neighbors. "Here," she said, and handed him the plant. "You could use some luck."

The man next to him wore the three stripes of a master sergeant, the highest rank a soldier could hold in the US Colored Troops. He was lying on his side. "Cinque" was sewn into the back of his shirt.

"Let me see where you're hurt, soldier."

"Just hold on. Need to find out about my men." He raised himself off the stretcher with his good arm. "You seen anyone from the marsh?"

"Not that anyone's said." She gently removed the blood-soaked dressing wrapped around his arm, but left the tourniquet up near his shoulder in place. His arm was nearly severed and there was no way to save it. The surgeons would use chloroform before sawing and he wouldn't feel it, and it was best to sedate a man prior to the final loss of an arm or leg. "You need something for pain?"

"Maybe later." Cinque scanned the faces of nearby soldiers. "Anyone here from the marsh?" he called. No one answered. He twisted his head to the other side in search of a familiar face. "You." He stared at a man whose wounds weren't apparent. "You all covered with mud. How long since you been at the fighting?"

The muddy man didn't answer.

"Don't mind him," she said. "Not sure he can hear you. Might not even be able to see you."

"Answer me, soldier," Cinque commanded. "That's an order."

"Some men, once they seen the elephant, can't see nothing else," Rachel said. "Some of them barely remember to blink their eyes. Nothing much nobody can do for him."

"She's right, seen the same thing after every battle," the soldier next to him said. A bandage covered the side of his head where his left ear used to be. "Think he stopped seeing and hearing after his buddy got disappeared by a cannonball. Ain't said nothing since."

"Where were you?" Cinque asked.

"Trapped near the crater with Corporal Freeman, sir." He added the "sir" when he saw the stripes on Cinque's sleeve. "At least we could fight back. Joe was leading us but we couldn't go nowhere. We was getting shot at from all sides, sir."

"Joe!" Rachel said. "Joe? You seen him? Does he have a whipping scar on his neck looking like a maple leaf?"

The man nodded. "Sound like the Joe I know. Every white officer was shot. Joe was leading all the men that could still move to the north side of the crater."

She grabbed onto the crude stretcher to steady herself. "He was alive?"

"Last I seen." The man cast his eyes down. "But ma'am? They was fighting their way out of a trap."

"How bad?" Cinque asked. "Don't remember nothing after the mine blew up. Ain't been nowhere else since—"

Rachel placed a hand on his uninjured forearm. "You'll get moved soon enough. Now quiet down and let this man tell me about my husband."

The man's eyes widened in wonder. "Rachel? You the one he been sending all them letters?"

"Haven't got any letters. But yes, I'm Rachel. Joe can write?"

This brought an eager nod. "And read some, too. He writes you every night."

"Is he okay? Please tell me he's still alive."

"Joe was up front," the man said, "after all the white officers was shot. Guess the Succesh figured the Colored Troops wouldn't know what to do." He looked at Cinque and Rachel with a level gaze, and came to attention as much as a man lying on a stretcher is able to. "Them Rebels figured wrong, sir. We got a lot of fighting to make up for, fought that much harder."

"What about Joe?" Rachel said.

"Like I said, last I seen he was leading all thems that didn't get shot." The soldier's eyes shifted away. "Wasn't many though. They was getting shot at from all sides. Taking a lot of cannon fire too. Not as bad as the marsh, maybe, but plenty bad."

"You're hurting my arm," Cinque said.

She released her hand, saw finger-shaped marks on his forearm. "Sorry. Forgot where I was." Then, to the soldier, "Tell me he's still alive. Please. At least tell me he had a way to stay alive."

The wounded soldier considered this, and finally said, "Plenty 'a cover on top of that hill. If they made it up there, got dug in, won't be no getting 'em off."

She reached inside herself, back to her memory of their childhood together, their special language and bond.

Turn and fight, Joe! Fight your way uphill!

CHAPTER TWENTY-TWO

Joe rested his finger on the trigger and surveyed each new position by looking down the barrel of his rifle. He led his men partway down the ridgeline, so the top of the hill offered protection from whomever was on the far side. Smoke and dust filled the valley and hid them from view below. Not ideal, but there wasn't a better place to reconnoiter.

Where you at, top eye? Sure could use you now. Which way would Rachel go?

The answer came to him by degrees, the way she promised it would. He trusted in God but kept moving; crawled forward a few more feet until he could see around the hill, crawled to the edge of the nearest ridge and peered around the rocky outcropping.

Eight Succesh soldiers crouched on the side of the hill. Joe crawled back, raised his arm and flashed four fingers twice, so the men close enough to see would know there were eight enemies nearby. Seven of his soldiers crawled forward to join him. Eight more took their places directly behind.

Joe peered down the barrel of his rifle at a Rebel soldier with sickly white skin so sunburned, most of it was peeled off. When pale blue eyes glanced in his direction, he squeezed the trigger. Seven more shots rang out almost as one when his men fired.

"Next line," he shouted. "Fire!"

Enough bullets pierced the mass of eight tangled bodies to remove any risk of a counterattack. "Well done, men," he called out. "Reload!"

He crawled forward and used the enemy bodies as a shield. Men shouted on the other side of the hill, but both sides spoke the same language and cursed with equal fluency.

"Shit!" he muttered, and scrambled back to his troops.

"What'd you see, sir?" the flag bearer asked.

"Firing positions," Joe ordered. "Cannons rolling this way! Cavalry, too. Maybe a hundred. Get ready." He held up his hand and motioned for the men to form a defensive position. He put his hands on the shoulders of the ones too scared to move. "Fear coming. But keep on with the firing."

"Fear coming, sir? Believe it already here." A soldier who took pride in his uniform had torn off the lower half of his shirt and wrapped it around his buddy's head as a bandage. His steady voice belied the terror in his eyes. "Must mean it time for firing."

The incessant thud of hoof beats meant the cavalry charge was in front of the cannons headed toward them. Staccato squeaks meant the wagons carrying the cannons were moving at a gallop.

"First two lines," Joe called out. "Shoot at the horses." Horses made large targets, and a cavalry soldier on foot was easier to fight. A cavalry soldier trapped beneath his horse, easier yet. He waited until the man next to him nodded in understanding and turned to pass the command down the line.

The charge was coming toward them much faster than he expected. The squeaks were much louder. He could hear the rattle of metal firing tools banging against the wagons. He didn't wait for nodded confirmation of his order, there wasn't time. "Next three lines," he bellowed, "shoot at the men!"

Nods came from behind him, but he didn't see them—his eyes focused on the hundred cavalry soldiers, close enough for him to make out their white faces. He shouted, "Get ready... Fire!"

A half-dozen of the lead horses fell under their bullets. The fallen horses tripped up the horses behind them. The initial charge slowed, but wasn't stopped. "Now! Fire at the men!" he screamed.

Three distinct volleys erupted. The cavalry charge became a mass of screaming, colliding bodies in a billowing cloud of dust, but Joe knew the cannons were right behind them.

At his command, the first two lines fired. The dust cloud made it impossible to see if their rounds wounded men or crippled horses, but none of the enemy emerged into the clearing. The charge was ended.

Crouching, Joe struggled to see through the dust cloud, knowing that if the cannons got off a shot, the next sound he heard might mean the death of all his men. *Got 'bout half a minute to decide which way to go. Being wrong means dying. Send me that top eye, Rachel. I'm fighting my way to you.*

"You bleeding, sir. Whole shirt's turning red." A different man was in charge of the company flag than when they marched into the battle.

"Most of it come from the man holding that flag before you," Joe said, though unless he tore his clothes off, he couldn't be sure. And there was no time.

Shots fired from Confederate cannons drowned out the flag bearer's reply, and both of them hit the dirt as percussive charges and canisters screamed over-head and thudded into the hill above them. *If anyone up there, they dead now,* Joe realized. *Succesh or Yankee, nobody gonna be alive after that much exploding.*

His thinking time was up. Time to make a decision on which way to move. The next volley could come at any second and this one might be on target. "Move out," he ordered. "We going uphill. Follow me."

Smoke and dust made coughing a part of breathing. He could tell his troops were behind him by the thud their boots made on the hard-packed ground. The man to his right swore when he tripped on a smoking bomb crater. The man on his left, old enough to be his father, wheezed from a lifetime spent breathing rice dust. Somewhere in the dusty cloud, a soldier screamed, the unnatural kind of scream a bullet knocks out of a man.

"Keep moving!" Joe ordered any man who faltered. When they were halfway up the hill he spotted a bomb crater, a place to dig in and make a stand. Maybe their last stand. Yelling, "Take cover!" he stepped aside and directed the men into the shallow hole. *This got to be where the shells landed,* he thought. *Cannon ain't gonna aim at the same place twice. Least I hope not—*

The remaining Succesh cavalry emerged from the dust cloud and galloped toward them. They were almost within firing range, leaving no time to organize the men into firing rows, only to reload. Joe took his place in front. "Men on my left, fire at the horses," he commanded. "Men on my right, fire at shoulder height when the horses is all the way down."

Loading his rifle calmed him some. He bit off the end of a paper cartridge and spit it toward the enemy. It gave him a moment to think, to call to the man beside him, "Fear coming, keep on with the firing."

"Fear coming, keep on firing," the man on his right repeated for the benefit of everyone within hearing range. "Fear coming, keep on firing," replaced the "Remember Fort Pillow" cry from earlier and was passed down the line.

Lord, Joe prayed, but no other words came. *Maybe I ain't got no business praying. What's there to pray for? Help me kill these men before they kill me? Don't figure God's listening to them kinda prayers.*

He fired instead of saying amen. "Reload!" he ordered.

"Keep on with the firing!" one soldier responded.

"Remember the slavers!" another man suggested. "They don't own me no more!" A new battle cry was adopted. "Remember the slavers," they shouted in unison. "They don't own me no more!" The men were outnumbered. The speed and superior maneuverability of the enemy's horses added to their disadvantage, but the US Colored Troops under his command had rage on their side. This rage sustained them while the hoof beats grew louder.

"Revenge!" he screamed, and aimed at the next white man he saw. The man was carrying a sword, an officer. *Good. One less slaver a nice use of this bullet.*

The horse galloped at full speed, so he allowed for the length of an extra stride, and fired. His shot was on target—the man was thrust backward and off the saddle—but the horse kept galloping and charged into the middle of their ranks. The man next to Joe lost half his face from horseshoes worn down to a razor-sharp edge.

Joe raised his rifle to ward off the flailing legs and thrust upward with his bayonet. He missed the screaming horse's legs and struck its heart. Blood poured from the horse's chest as it fell on top of him. He struggled to crawl out from beneath the horse but he was wedged against the side of the bomb crater and the horse's ribcage, his rifle entangled in the bridle. One of his boots was trapped by the saddle and he couldn't wiggle it free. *Ankle must be broke. Way it hurts so much when I twist it.*

His men were outnumbered three to one, but fought until they ran out of ammunition. His pride in them was mixed with angry helplessness; he was forced to watch the battle turn against them while he was trapped beneath the horse. The stand-in flag bearer raised his hands in surrender. The Succesh shot him. Rebel soldiers shot three more of Joe's men while they held their hands up in surrender. Joe closed his eyes and pretended to be dead. *What else can I do? Can't fight, might as well be dead. No point in saying nothing. Surrendering the same as dying.*

He heard the Rebel commander order his troops to look for and execute survivors. He unbuttoned his bloody shirt and pulled it open so part of it was visible, let the flies settle on his face and clenched his jaw against flinching at their feathery touches. His side hurt where a bullet grazed him, but he could breathe without a gurgle and he didn't feel cold. Most of the men he'd held while they bled to death complained of cold.

A noise above him made him hold his breath, waiting for a bullet to end his life. The shadow of death, lurking within a Rebel soldier, passed him by. He released the breath and listened, and after a while, heard only silence.

His legs ached from being trapped beneath the horse and he was certain his ankle got pulled a little farther from his leg each time he tried to twist it free. He kept trying until he passed out from the pain.

He came to hungry and thirsty, realized the dust cloud had cleared. Slanting light told him it was late afternoon. The pain continued to alternate between aches and deep throbbing, and he couldn't remember if he'd ever felt worse, but most of all, he felt like a coward. His last thought before he again lost consciousness was wondering what would kill him first: a Rebel patrol or being left on the field.

Both Union and Confederate armies accepted the coming darkness as terms for a cease-fire. When the last injury was bandaged and the wounded made as comfortable as the crude field hospital would allow, Rachel donned her Quaker bonnet, pinned a red ribbon to her blouse and picked up her lantern. There would be no measured path tonight; she started directly for the hill where Joe was last seen. While she walked, she tried to steel herself that Joe might have perished in the fierce battle and never made it to the hilltop. If so, she would accept that as her ultimate punishment for Samuel's death. But hope was a stubborn thing. There must be a chance, there had to be a chance Joe still lived. This was a war about second chances. If a man could summon up a cough or a moan, he might be saved. A whimper or faint gasp for breath might be all that stood between life and death for someone left on the battlefield, and if this someone were Joe, she would find him.

In her haste, she might have been less diligent about checking for signs of life if it was a Succesh white boy, but who could blame her? She wasn't the angel of death, but she wasn't an angel, either.

She put her ear to the chest of a US Colored Soldier and listened for a long time, time enough to give his heart plenty of chances to let her know it still beat.

She held a mirror up to his face in case any breath remained in his body. Next, she pressed the palm of her hand against the man's nose and mouth to feel for heat, breath, any sign of life. *A man who manages to fight his way free of slavery deserves every chance at life.*

She stood, held her lantern at chest height and watched the flies. A curious moth was drawn to the flame. Swarms of flies weren't so nervous around dead people, but moths didn't have that much sense. Some ventured too close and sizzled against the lamp's hot metal base. Some flared into smoke with a burst of bright light if they wandered into the flaming wick. The larger the moth, the brighter they burned.

The moth singed one of its wings and fluttered haphazardly. When it tried to land on her nose, she put her lantern on the ground and used both arms to shoo it away. The wounded moth saved a young man's life. From her standing position, his faint breathing would have been too faint for her to hear, but when she bent over to pick up the lantern, it moved her close enough to hear his weak gasp.

A tattered flag, blue and white but mostly red with blood, stuck to his chest. The man, a boy really, opened his eyes when she peeled the banner away, moved his lips but no words came out. She turned toward camp so they could see her lantern swinging side to side. The answering signal meant the stretcher-bearers were on their way.

"Here," she said. "Try and drink this." She pulled her canteen from her haversack and poured a few drops of water onto his lips. He was too weak to sit up, but not too weak to swallow. Encouraged, she gave him a drink of water a few patient drops at a time so he wouldn't choke, placed a dampened towel on his forehead, knelt beside him and waited for the stretcher to arrive. Exhaustion bordering on despair bowed her head until it looked as though she were kneeling in prayer, but she was merely resting. She'd found one soldier still alive. There might be others. She might find Joe.

One of the stretcher-bearers was a soldier she'd found late at night, alone and near death, but too stubborn to die on an abandoned battlefield. "You all right, Miss Rachel?" he asked.

"Just resting." She grasped the offered hand and allowed herself to be helped up. "Thank you."

"Yes, Miss Rachel. We'll get him to the hospital." His smile shone bright in the lamplight. "Be back soon as we can. Still watching for your lantern. Looking for the next wave."

Seeing his smile, she realized she was being selfish in hurrying past so many bodies on her way to the hill. What if, in her haste, she missed someone else who deserved a second chance, someone just like Joe? She nodded her goodbye, then raised the lantern to shoulder height and held it as far from her body as her arm would reach. Slowly, she pivoted in a circle. In this way she moved from body to body. At times she overlapped but never exceeded the lantern's reach. Some bodies were so hideously disfigured there was no need to move closer.

After two or three revolutions, she kept still and listened for a faint moan or forlorn cough. She didn't move until the crickets chirped. Crickets got nervous and stayed quiet if wounded men moved nearby.

A noise too faint to identify came to her ears. *Was that a cough?* "Hello out there," she called. "Can you hear me?"

Brief flashes of green from lightning bugs arced over the battlefield the way falling stars streak across the sky on a new-moon night. A thin green tendril of light led her to the wreckage of a cannon and a team of horses. Enemy soldiers lay nearby, some of them boys. The Confederate Army had put rifles in their hands and sent them off to die in defense of slavery, but she'd seen slaves much younger killed for no good reason.

She turned away and finished the circle, listened, let her top eye guide her, and followed the gentle nudge that suggested she look on the back side of the hill. In the moonlight, a horse lay on its side. It would take precious time to climb the hill. *Should I go look now? Or should I move on?* "Hello? Anybody up there?"

No answer. Either someone who needed help was too weak to be heard or they were already dead. She sighed. The only way to find out was to climb.

Winged sumac grew near the top of the hill. A few clusters of greenish-yellow flowers clung to the shrub, but most of its blossoms had been knocked to the ground. Lightning bugs blinked on and off where a few leaves still clung to the branches. *When the lightning bugs are taller'n you, means it's time for bed,* Grandma used to say. *If I ever got the chance to lay down on a real bed, I'd probably sleep for a year. Bet I wouldn't—*

She stopped climbing and held her breath.

What was that? Somebody moaning? Or just my mind playing tricks on me from being so tired?

She held still and let her top eye guide her. The crickets remained silent but lightning bugs showed her the way. Near a bomb crater, behind the bullet-riddled corpse of a Confederate soldier, a man lay face down. The ground muffled his weakened moans and ragged breathing. A trail of blood led from the bomb crater to where she found him. It was a good sign; it meant he was a fighter. She waved her lantern. The stretcher-bearers gave an answering wave.

She set the lantern on the ground and gently rolled the corpse away so she could tend to the injured man trapped underneath. His foot was twisted the wrong way on his left ankle. Drag marks in the ground showed where he'd crawled away from the crater, and the path he took to get this far. He was lying in a small patch of clover, and the lantern's light illuminated his hand. He clutched a plant with four leaves. The sight made her smile. Grandma could always find a four-leaf clover in a field full of threes. *Just like her to use lightning bugs or clover to help me find this poor soldier. Just wish her top eye would help me find Joe.*

His clothes were disheveled and dirty, his shirt stained with blood. Despair made her close her eyes for a moment. There was little she could do for someone shot in the stomach, other than make them comfortable. Her haversack held enough morphine to take away the pain from any wound.

"Can you breathe? You shot in the chest? The neck?" When he didn't reply, she reached for the lantern to move it closer to his head. "Can you hear me? Where you hurt?"

If he lived this long, he deserved to see the sky once more before the morphine took away his consciousness. She carefully rolled him onto his back.

"Rachel." Another feeble whisper. "Hold on, Rachel. I'se close coming."

"Oh my God. Joe?" She moved the lantern so light shined directly onto his face. A scar in the shape of a maple leaf formed a dark blemish on his neck. It was him.

She closed her eyes and thanked God with a prayer so sincere it didn't need words. Then she scrambled to her feet and frantically waved her lantern. The metal handle rattled from the force and the flame fluttered from the rush of air as she desperately swung it back and forth. The stretcher-bearers were returning from the field hospital; she could see them about halfway through the battleground. Fearing they wouldn't see her up on the hill, she twisted the wick as high as it would go, barely feeling where the heated metal burned her fingers.

"Help," she screamed, flailing the lantern over her head. "Over here. Hurry!"

Their lantern swung in response. "Is you okay Miss Rachel?" one of them called out. When there was no answer, they started to run. She didn't hear them because she'd dropped to the ground to look closer at Joe. The longest minutes of her life began.

Joe's lips were parched and peeling, his cheeks drawn, his eyes hazed over and sunken in his head, the eyes of a dying man. Her love for him mixed with the fear of losing him and the healer in her faltered. The panic of not knowing what to do brought a harsh sob from her throat, then another.

More healing in knowing a person care, Grandma reminded her. *"Caring more powerful than tonic. Remember, child. Body heals itself, mostly. Just got to help it along...*

Something clicked in her mind "Thirsty," she sobbed, and scrambled around in her haversack. "Course you wanting for water, you been in the sun all day."

She dropped to her knees beside him and pulled out the canteen. "Hold on, Joe," she sobbed.

He coughed, but managed a few sips before pushing the canteen aside. "Let me hold you, Rachel. Let me dream 'bout us being together." The effort made him lose his breath, and his upper body went limp.

"Don't give up," she wailed. "Fight! C'mon Joe, fight back." *Oh God!* she prayed. *I'll do anything.* "Joe! Don't leave me, Joe." *Oh God. Please!* She lifted his head and rested it on her knees, forced him to drink a bit more before he shook his head and pushed the canteen away with his chin.

"We in heaven, Rachel? We finally together? Grandma and Samuel was waiting on me. They told me—"

"No," she wailed. "You ain't in heaven. I'm alive. You still alive. You hear me? You alive! You got to live, Joe. Hang on to life. I know you got it in you. I always knowed it."

He reached for her. "I'se cold. Feel the cold north wind blowing right on through me."

"Hold on, Joe. You gonna be okay."

"This a dream? Keep having the same one. We together when I dream. Or is this heaven? Be glad if it is. Maybe I won't have to hurt no more ... if you and little Samuel is with me—"

"I'm real, Joe. We together. Finally. We made it. You hear me? We made it! You hold on. I'm gonna get you well. I got Grandma's hands, a healer's hands." *I won't let you die!*

Joe's arms slid from around her. "Afraid to wake up," he said. "Too much hurt in you not being there when I do."

"You hold on, Joe. I ain't lettin' go. I promise."

"Awful cold. Sorry," he struggled to swallow. "Loved you so long. I'm sorry."

She held him tighter and leaned her mouth to his ear. "We together, Joe. You just hold on. We're together now, and free."

CHAPTER
TWENTY-THREE

After the spring rains of 1865, streams near Perrysville, Kentucky ran pure once more. Rachel and Joe crossed a small creek at a shallow ford where bright green grass flourished beneath an outcropping of pale gray limestone. Pure spring water still flowed from beneath a jumbled pile of rocks and filled a series of shallow pools. The water settled in Rachel's empty stomach with a familiar sense of heaviness. Joe noticed a slight mineral taste in the water from the lower pools. They set up a squirrel trap beneath a huge oak tree and followed a faint path leading toward an abandoned plantation house.

The grass was greenest over the burial mounds that honored and sheltered the fallen men from both sides. Dignity was restored to the unfortunate men killed in battle; proper tombstones now rested where row upon row of white fence posts once stood. Silver-lace vines twisted and twirled around crumbling chimneys. Fireweed spread over the misshapen ruins of the great house and softened the harsh scorch marks with tiny purple blossoms.

The decrepit slave quarters remained standing, but their pronounced lean was new. The tattered roof and red-streaked walls gave the shack an abandoned look. *Had the two women moved on?* Rachel tossed a rock against the side of the dilapidated house. *Not sure if I'm announcing my arrival or checking for ghosts.*

"Who's there?" A woman with sightless eyes felt her way onto the front porch. She kept her arms in front of her and shuffled toward the railing that surrounded the porch.

"It's me," Rachel said. "Remember the squirrels I brought last time?"

"Is you that woman with the baby?"

"Brought my husband this time." She put her hands behind her back and changed the subject. "Is your mother still alive?"

"Barely. We ain't got nothing to eat, but you might as well come on inside."

"This is my husband, Joe Freeman," is how Rachel introduced Joe to the two women.

"Mighty pleased to meet you," Joe took off his hat. "Rachel nursed me back from dead. Must mean she can heal anybody."

"Got your work cut out for you," the ancient woman said. She was bedridden and propped up against the wall so she could breathe.

"She started feeling poorly 'bout the time we run out of firewood," her daughter explained. She turned sightless eyes in Rachel's direction. "You saved us."

Rachel nodded. "You saved yourselves, helped me, too. Glad I can return the favor."

"Sounds like our prayers been answered." The old lady coughed until she ran out of breath.

"Yes, ma'am. Guess that's true for all of us." Rachel moved to her bedside. "You tell me what hurts."

"Faster tellin you what don't." Her toothless grin was cut short by another coughing spell.

When the spasms ended, Rachel said, "I been collecting herbs and such. Adding hope and freedom makes for a powerful tonic." She patted the leather pouch on her hip. "Joe made me this. Sure to be something in here for what's ailing you."

"This mean we having squirrel for supper?" the daughter asked.

Rachel grinned. "If they ain't smartened up none."

"Might take me longer to get there." Joe waved his crutches by way of explanation.

"Spoon in the same place."

"I'll be down in a while, Joe." Rachel said. "Help you carry the water back."

"We still got all that rope—"

"You made," her daughter finished when her mother started coughing again.

Rachel opened the flap on her medicine pouch, started rummaging around. "Once we get that cough cleared up, switchels will get you outta bed and moving around in no time."

"Switchels?"

"Like a tonic. Any fruit juice with some vinegar in it."

"Where you getting vinegar?"

"From cider. Most any fruit will make cider. Leave it out long enough, turns to vinegar every time."

"Told you she was a healer," Joe bragged. "She done nursing in the war."

"Is it over?" the daughter asked. "We ain't heard no fighting in a long time—"

"But we ain't had no visitors in longer," her mother finished

"War's over," he pointed to his uniform. "North won."

"But we still in the South." Rachel rested the back of her hand against the ancient woman's forehead.

"Why we headed north. Get this fever to break, taking you with us."

"And we ain't stopping till we get there." Joe put the spoon in his pocket and wound the rope handle of the bucket around one of his crutches. He turned around to head for the door—

"Hold on," the daughter called out.

He looked over his shoulder. "What's the matter?"

"Thought you was Peg Leg Joe when I heard you coming. Figured I was hearing things. Maybe not. You on crutches?"

"Yes, ma'am. But not forever. Not with a healer good as Rachel. Always know when it gonna rain, though."

"Let me help, then. You be my eyes. I'll be your arms. Figure we both be moving 'bout the same speed: slow."

Joe laughed. "Long as it ain't dead slow."

Over a breakfast of squirrel stew, Joe and Rachel tried to explain how colored people in the South weren't really free. August 1865, three months after the Confederate surrender, a hostile invading army occupied the South to enforce a foreign law of emancipation. It would take more than defeat for the landed ruling class to relinquish the cheap labor so critical for its continued existence. The new President, Andrew

Johnson, a southerner himself, granted pardons to southern sympathizers. He also looked the other way when racist laws were instituted, and vetoed legislation intended to give ex-slaves the freedoms promised by his predecessor. There were no jobs, and the Black Codes made it a crime to be unemployed. Violators were sentenced to hard labor in the fields they once worked as slaves. The pay was the same: nothing.

"Last year's beans," is how Joe explained the food shortage. "Ain't no way to grow enough beans for both the man working the land and the man owning it, without sharing. Most big-house men would rather starve than share."

"Thought the war was gonna change that," the ancient woman's cough was almost gone. "Don't make no sense."

"Maybe people in the South been living a lie for so long, it's passing for truth. Law don't change nothing if nobody following it." Rachel looked outside and watched as a lazy V, outlined against the deep-water blue of a cloudless sky, dissolved and reformed with a different bird at the tip. "Cranes know when it's time to head north."

"Time for us to leave, too." Joe pushed himself up. After four weeks of healing, Joe's ankle was weak, but he managed with a cane now. "I'll go check on the squirrel traps and get us some water. Feel a storm coming."

Rachel helped the ancient woman out of bed. "Let's see 'bout getting you dressed."

It rained later that afternoon. They didn't let a little bad weather stop them. Travel was a hardship, but none of them wanted to spend an extra minute in a southern prison because of bad weather. "Rain for forty days and forty nights for all I care," the ancient woman said. She sat in the narrow cart Joe built for her from an abandoned Rebel cannon. There were two long handles for Joe to stand between so he could pull. Rachel pushed, and the ancient woman's sightless daughter kept one hand on the cart as she walked alongside.

They moved north and it was a slow journey, but a healer is welcome in every town. Sometimes a meal or shelter for the night, people shared what they had and made do without what they needed. In these troubled times, most freed slaves were destitute. Such poverty was an equalizer, for when everyone was poor, sharing was accepted as part of life. No one starved; no one feasted either. In a countryside decimated by war, squirrels managed to survive, so squirrel stew became the staple. Rachel's knowledge of plants meant there was always something added.

"Called these 'stretchers' in the Army. Can't remember eating this much rabbit food, though." Joe stripped the leaves and cut away the stalks from unopened sunflower buds. When cooked, and with a little imagination, they tasted like artichokes.

"Poke salad give me the gas something awful. Ain't complaining, mind you," the mother added. "Take forever to chew without no teeth, that's all."

"Roasted acorns with a little bacon fat takes some getting used to," the daughter allowed. "But it's close enough to coffee for drinking."

"Called these 'eggs on the march.' " Joe placed fresh eggs on their bottoms in the ashes of the morning fire. "Cooked in their shells makes them easy to carry."

They traveled at night, partly from habit, mostly to avoid the heat and the locals. They followed the narrow animal trails that wound their way through the forests. "Never thought I'd be crossing the Kentucky River again, but here we are," Joe said. "It's how I floated free."

"Nothing but pain and sorrow here for me," Rachel said, gazing at the river. "Can't see nothing but graves." A granite marker sat atop the mass grave where Confederate and Union soldiers now rested together.

"Some machines get so broke, there ain't no fixing 'em." Joe brushed his fingers against the marker and cocked his head to the side. "Could be some people like a worn-out machine. They so broke, there ain't no fixing 'em, can't live together—maybe dying together the best they can do." He lowered his head and looked away.

Rachel recognized the dazed expression of a soldier who's wrestled with the demons of war and lost. She kept still and listened to a Kentucky warbler sing a bitter-sweet aria while Joe found his way back from troubled memories. She had troubling memories of her own. A lone pin oak was visible in the distance. She put her hands behind her back and gazed inwardly upon her own demons.

"Look over there, Rachel." Joe pointed toward a small creek. "Hollyhocks. They growing all around that big tree. Remember how much your Grandma loved hollyhocks?"

Rachel nodded but hung her head. She couldn't get past her guilt to appreciate the beauty of Grandma's favorite flowers.

"Dreamt of you every night," Joe said, "about the only thing ever give me any peace. Dreamed some of Samuel and your Grandma, too. They was usually all colored-up: Samuel in blue and your Grandma wearing all the colors in the rainbow—just like that scarf she always had around her neck."

Rachel clenched her hands into fists until her fingernails bit into the palms of her hands, but all she felt was the tender skin of Samuel's face and the blood he coughed up from not being able to breathe. She unclenched her fists, intertwined her fingers to ease the cramps, but her hands wouldn't keep still. If she closed her eyes, the memory of Samuel's murder haunted her. If she dared raise her head, the view was of her baby's gravesite.

Joe put his arms around her and held her hands in his own. He had calloused palms and crooked fingers from a lifetime of hard work and fixing things, but his hands were gentle. He held Rachel in his arms, didn't let go of her hands while she confessed to killing their child in order to survive.

"I blame myself for not being there," he said. "How can you ever forgive me?"

The Devil still owned the next stretch of road. Makeshift cemeteries and piles of rubble were all that remained of the Confederate saloons and brothels, but Rachel recognized the tree stumps with their gnarled roots reaching toward the sky like skeletal fingers. The same sticky mud clung to the bottoms of her shoes and she got taller with every step.

"Nothing but bounty hunters and pattyrollers around here," she said. "These people as mean as the swamp they come out of. I passed this way with Hercules and Aveta. Never thought I'd be coming through here again."

A canal cut through the middle of the swamp. She watched a barge heaped with coal enter a lock. Water foamed beneath the hull as the river rushed to fill the void.

"Last time I came this way, had a bounty hunter looking for me. Right about here is where I run out of trees to hide behind. Stayed all crouched over the rest of the way."

"Learned about standing up straight in the Army," Joe said. "Ain't felt the need to slouch since."

"Just be glad to be standing," the ancient woman said. "Glad I can get outta this cart when we stop."

"Been hearing birds I ain't never heard before." Her daughter cupped a hand behind her ear.

"Golden finches," Rachel said. "They look like little streaks of yellow when they fly—or maybe the way a bright sun feels on your face," she added, remembering the woman couldn't see.

"I can imagine that." She sniffed. "Ain't complaining, but I sure thought the North would smell better." What she lost in sight she gained back in other senses. "There a sewer near here?"

"Part of the Miami and Erie Canal. Runs right through Cincinnati," Rachel said. "Used to smell worse, when the Contraband Camp was nearby. Ain't there no more, though."

"Where we gonna live, then?" the daughter asked

"North of there."

Joe cocked his head and looked at her the way he did when he was thinking. "North? Or The North?"

She shrugged. "North as you want to go."

"All the way to Canady, Rachel?" the ancient woman asked. "The Promised Land?"

"Maybe. Going as far north as it takes."

"There really such a place?" the daughter asked. "Been hearing 'bout 'the North' all my life. Been hanging on to the dream for so long, don't know how to feel when it's coming true."

Rachel gently squeezed the daughter's shoulder. "Ain't got to let go of your dreams. Just grab on to the real. When we get on that ferry boat up ahead, won't be stopping until the north side of the Ohio River. No more South from there on out. That's what real."

"And if it ain't far enough," Joe promised, "we'll keep going till it is."

"Feel like I gone to heaven without dying." Tears curved down the wrinkles in the ancient woman's face and dripped onto her blouse. Rachel noticed, tapped Joe's shoulder, and they brought the cart to a stop.

"What wrong with your voice, Mama? You crying?"

"Not from hurt, child," she replied. "I been hearing talk about tears of joy all my life. Never believed in 'em till now."

Joe reached for Rachel's hand. "Knew I had to get free when I felt you praying for me the night you left."

"And every night since." She leaned her head on his shoulder. "Didn't stop praying just because the sun came up. Asked Grandma to watch out for you, too." Her tears were part joy and part hurt, but this time she didn't try to stop them. She could feel again. She missed Samuel, but she was with Joe.

If the price of being happy is feeling a little pain, seems like a fair trade for not feeling nothing at all.

CHAPTER
TWENTY-FOUR

Dear Friends: We made it to Canady, so I take this opportunity of wrighting a few lines to let you know we are in good health and safe. Hoping a few lines may find you enjoying the same blessing. We rode the train all the way to Detroit where we hid in Mr. Finneys barn while the pattyrollers chasing us drink in his saloon upstairs. We take the 2nd Baptist Church boat across Detroit River to Sandwich Church in Amherstburg,

Canady. We sing as we step off the T. Whitney boat and stand on Canady ground.

No sine of Rachel yet, but our prayers are for her arrival. Hercules goes to work this morning for Mr. Dentons and Aveta is open a shop for sewing.

> Yours with respect,
> Richard Dentons, writing for:
> Hercules X
> Aveta X

Deacon Turner held the letter above his head. "The Lord has answered our prayers! People we been praying for are truly free. We was all praying for Rachel's safe return. Now she's back here with us. Brought her husband, Joe, and two more, besides."

"Amen!" the congregation of the Cincinnati African Methodist Episcopalian church replied. Some knew of the escape, others didn't recognize the names, but all could rejoice at the prospect of a couple reunited.

Rachel blinked away the tears in her eyes. Joe squeezed her hand and kept his eyes shut so he wouldn't cry.

After church and Sunday lunch, Rachel and Joe sat next to Deacon Turner as he maneuvered his wagon through the busy streets. She counted each turn of the squeaking wheels as another step closer to finally feeling free.

"Look up there," Joe pointed toward the horizon. "See that cloud way over there? The one with all the colors? Kinda reminds me of that sash Grandma always wore."

"Me too, won't never forget that sash—or how much love Grandma had to give."

He was quiet for a moment, then gave a sheepish smile. "I know it sounds crazy, but I could of sworn I actually seen Grandma a couple a times. Back during our troubles."

She lowered her eyes to his. "Like when you needed more help than anybody could give?"

"Something like that. Like I said, sound a little crazy. I know she been gone for, what … five years now?"

"I seen her, too," she admitted. "Seen her temper when a tree I was hiding under got struck by lightning. Heard her watching over me when there was thunder for three days. One time, when things was the worst, I swear she put her hand on my shoulder and made me promise to keep living."

His smile widened. "Guess you and me had our own guardian angel."

Deacon Turner noticed their smiles. "If she's in heaven where she belongs, she ought to be feeling pretty good right about now."

Rachel squeezed Joe's hand. "I expect so. And I never thought I'd be riding high on a wagon on a city street instead of hiding in the alleys."

"Drive my wagon where I wants to go." Deacon Turner let go of the reins. "Looky there. Mules know the way cause we been down the main street so many times."

"Glad it's not a boat," Rachel said.

"Or a river," Joe added.

Rachel smiled, but it was only on the surface. There was no escape from her memory. Mr. Lincoln kept his promise that they could be free, only it wasn't his land anymore. *Joe and I lost our child and nobody cares, but let one white man die because of slavery and the whole nation wears black.*

"No point looking back when we got so much ahead." Joe reached for Rachel's hands, held them over his heart until she looked into his eyes. In the unspoken language of their shared thoughts, they vowed, *our next child will grow up loved. And free*

ABOUT THE AUTHOR

 A research grant to explore the Underground Railroad in Kentucky is what inspired this book. Stephen Brown is currently working on his third novel. He lives in Kentucky and travels throughout the state on behalf of the Kentucky Humanities Council Speakers Bureau.

For more information go to:
www.singingrockpublishing.com

Made in the USA
Charleston, SC
21 January 2015